WIRETAP!

WIRETAP!

CHARLES EINSTEIN

CUTTING EDGE

ISBN-13: 978-1-962896-52-8

Published by
Cutting Edge Books
PO Box 8212
Calabasas, CA 91372
www.cuttingedgebooks.com

CHAPTER ONE

THE NAME OF THE CITY WAS AIMERLY. IT WAS A SMALL city in the northeast, surrounded by traditions but without a tradition of its own. It could claim a dominant influence neither British nor French nor Dutch, nor Primitive New England. Perhaps the phrase *American Frontier* might here be loosely applied, for once this had been a canal town—that was its reason for being. But long since, the canal had been diverted, and through parts of what had been the bed of the waterway, the railroad ran now; the tracks there all by themselves, lit by lone and solemn signal eyes of red and green, without houses on either side until almost the center of the town.

Yet in the absence of any tradition, still it was a picture, a strange Still Life America, the night Judge Yorty fell dead, falling there so that his body was half in the street, half on the raised wooden porch of the Kamm Hotel, a porch that served also as the sidewalk in that stretch of eighty feet where it fronted Rain Street. Two o'clock in the morning it was—the moon small but livid-bright in the sky, its light begetting a color complementary to the dark, uneven red-brick paving of the wide street.

From the porch, there were four entrances to the hotel: the main entrance, another that was little more than a side door at the north end, and then the barbershop and the drugstore, both unnecessarily ornate without being overly so, both having rear doorways that led to the hotel lobby. It was through the small auxiliary door at the north end of the porch that the old judge came. He paused there for a moment, seeming to lean his body in the direction of the street light some forty feet away, and faintly in that light, more noticeably in the light from the moon, the old gold railroad watch glistened dully as he took it out to see the time. Then he looked both ways, then began walking south along the porch, past the barbershop and the drugstore.

From the railroad two blocks away there was the dirty metallic sound of a fast freight, eighty cars or more, twin diesels already long out of sight and gone. It was a rattling sound, the sound of empty freight cars and wheels clacking over the switch points beyond the depot.

The other sound, the sound of the gunfire, could have come from anywhere. It chased itself echo for echo, so no one could say there had been four shots instead of two, or one instead of three. It spun the judge, caught him, set him into a kind of ballet; his right knee drew up, his left hand groped for his middle. His right hand shot outward, fingers splayed apart, but missed the old termite-ridden porch pillar, and—first shoulder, then head— the upper half of his body fell into the street. In the light of the moon Judge Yorty's hat rolled away in a little wobbly half circle, and came to rest upside down like a beggar's in the middle of Rain Street.

After that there was quiet again, and no lights came alive in the windows of the hotel; after a time another fast freight, this one going the other way, hammered the center of the town and was gone.

It was a law—one of the rather few laws that separate man from the lesser animals: Never shoot a judge. Now it had been violated, and yet in the city of Aimerly, nerve center of Aimerly County wherein Judge Yorty's jurisdiction lay, no man could be found who in his heart could say he wanted to know who the killer was. Next day's edition of the Aimerly *Times* proclaimed solemnly the police theory that the killing was the work of The Syndicate. And yet The Syndicate, if there was such a thing, would be the last of all to kill a judge. If you thought it through, which nobody ever did, you realized that to say that the underworld had done this deed was to say that the old judge was something of a criminal in his own right. Perhaps he had sent some racketeers to jail in his time, as indeed he had; perhaps he was sitting on some unfavorable probation reports, as indeed he was; perhaps he could hold over a man's head a suspended sentence from years gone by, as indeed he could. But why kill him—unless he tried to use these elements for private shakedown purposes? And what nice, kindly old judge, beloved of the community as the *Times* declared Elbert Yorty to be, would do a thing like that?

No, The Syndicate, if there was such a thing, operated under a code of justice that in many respects matched its more public counterparts of law enforcement. There is an old saying in the law: Equity will not issue a decree it can not enforce. This enforcement was the job, and the reason for being, of the boss racketeer.

In Aimerly County, the boss racketeer was by name Andrew Fannell. He had a criminal record dating back to prohibition, and thus it was in his nephew's name that he operated the Holiday Inn, a swank roadhouse on Seven Mile Highway, the road that led from Aimerly City to Forest Downs, the race track.

But if you were to take Andy Fannell alongside any civic leader in Aimerly, and compare them in terms of their honesty and probity, you were in for a tough time. If you were to rate them on a compass where the truth lay due north, Fannell was no worse than west-southwest. Joe Thomas, the county prosecutor and the leading officer of law enforcement, was no better than due east and not coming up any. Ben Phillips, who had moved into town some years ago and now owned a string of liquor stores and was running for alderman in the impending local election, was a pretty stuffy northwest. Damn close to due south was Harry Millburn, a private detective who knew the fascinating, frightening mechanics of eavesdropping. He was useful to many men and available to all.

He was especially in demand right now. Aimerly had money. Aimerly was one of the first communities to go over to the national pattern being established by the telephone company, whereby eventually any phone could connect to any other phone anywhere in the country merely by dialing. In the new pattern, the first three of a phone number's seven digits had to be set so that they would fit the national code and yet not duplicate any other similar exchange. You could not, for example, dial ANdover 3 and BOulevard 3 in the same area, because the digits were mechanically the same—2-6-3—the 2 corresponding on the dial to the A of ANdover and the B of BOulevard; the 6 corresponding to the N of ANdover and the O of BOulevard.

And so when Aimerly changed over, in the scheme of things all of its phones went on two dial exchanges—MAin 3 and PRospect 4. This in turn brought about a certain period of upheaval at the headquarters of the telephone company, the big non-mechanical change being the switching over from operator's call and billing slips to the machine devices that would take over the handling of these records.

The reaction on the public was predictable. There was a certain upswing in the number of crank complaints to the police about phones being tapped. That helped make it a particularly good time to really tap a phone, if you felt like it.

Joe Thomas, the district attorney, felt like it. He could tap any phone he wanted to. All he had to do was get a legal tap order signed by a judge, and Judge Yorty would sign anything Joe handed to him. But Thomas, like many county prosecutors who operate away from the biggest cities, had a private law practice on the side. It became important for him to seek phone-tapped information on behalf of some clients without doing it as a regular police procedure. For this reason, Thomas had one of his law partners contact Harry Millburn, the private detective, who in turn acted as "tap broker" and helped set up what the papers later would call the "tap nest." Millburn was told that the job was a confidential police job. He was told this for two reasons—one reason was that it would be easier for him to enlist the help of a phone company man in hooking into the main connection or frame at phone company headquarters; the other was that if he ever traced the job back to Thomas, Thomas would have this as protection. From time to time the police did run a wiretap outside normal police tap channels—cops checking up on other cops.

But there was no reason to suppose Millburn would seek, or be able, to trace the source of this assignment. There was even less reason to suppose anybody would ever find out about the tap nest.

Thomas put a tap on six phones—one for divorce information, the others for industrial espionage. But the tap nest was so constituted that it could have cut in on any phone in the Aimerly area. This was all right with Thomas, what with election time coming up. The worst that could happen would be that somebody at the phone company would get wind of the operation and tell the police, but the police might be chary of making any arrests under such circumstances, and even then it would be tough to trace back to Thomas, and even then he was still county prosecutor. So the worst that could happen would be that the operation would be knocked out. If it came to a crisis, Joe Thomas could always display a legal tap order signed by a judge.

Of course, that was the thing of it. Judge Yorty would know about it, but now he was dead. He was a smart fellow, the old judge. He knew more things about more people than anybody else in town. He knew where every body lay except his own.

CHAPTER TWO

THE DEATH OF THE JUDGE WAS NOT TOTALLY DISPLEASING to Joe Thomas, the county prosecutor. It was certainly not totally displeasing to Ben Phillips, who was running against the Thomas machine in the race for alderman. Although this was the only municipal office being contested in the election, it carried with it majority control of the Board of Aldermen, and Phillips seized on the killing of the judge as a major issue.

But if two such stalwart anti-crime figures as Thomas and Phillips were not particularly displeased by the death of the judge, the state anti-crime commission, its headquarters a hundred miles away in Port Gerard, the state capital, was absolutely delighted. The anti-crime commission, a private, citizen-supported body, regarded deaths—certain deaths—as manna from heaven. If a political or underworld figure was killed, the papers would invariably raise great hue and cry. Since the only weapon the anti-crime commission had at its disposal was publicity, it rushed in where the angels were busily treading on a new corpse. It was a labor murder in New York, for example, that enabled the anti-crime committee there to bring about publicity that exposed trotting-track scandals and prison irregularities. Once you got publicity, one thing led to another with consummate ease. The thing was to get the publicity to begin with. Murder was the best catalyst.

Now, with the death of the judge, the anti-crime commission in Port Gerard moved fast. Walter Lord, managing director

CHARLES EINSTEIN

of the commission, called in his best man, a sad-faced former detective named Sam Murray, and told him to get up to Aimerly.

"Take five hundred dollars," Lord said to Murray. "Spend it for information."

"Where?" Murray said. "Traveler's Aid?"

"I don't give a goddam where. And don't play Nero Wolfe. We don't give a damn who shot the judge. What we're interested in was those tap orders he signed."

"Oh, yes," Murray said. "Expose wiretapping and perhaps the state legislature will investigate and then we will have strict new wiretapping laws. It will be illegal to tap another man's phone if he is a confessed sodomist who was bitten by a whale in the South Atlantic on a Tuesday. Otherwise, it'll be okay."

"You didn't look so cynical last night," Lord said.

"How do you know?"

"I heard from a fella who saw you at one of those places on the hill—soft lights, pretty music, and conning a broad around."

"I like girls," Murray said. "Would you prefer me otherwise?"

In fact, Murray did like girls—except show girls. He had been married to a show girl once, a girl named Edna, and she had run him into the ground and divorced him with speed and dispatch. Murray was only thirty-four now. He looked older.

"Only three things you have to remember about Aimerly," Lord said.

"You mean there's only three things you know about Aimerly," Murray said to him.

Lord ignored the remark. "Number one, Aimerly is Andy Fannell's town. He's got the roadhouse and the race track and he's the boss of the warehouse loaders' union—you know, the platform men. He's probably branched out into trucking by now. Number two, the first place to go is the paper there. The publisher's name is Leclerc. He runs the television station, too. Talk to him. Number three, I've made a contact for you with a guy named Harry Millburn. He's a private detective and a tap expert. He can tell you something. What, I don't know. All I know about him is the name and the reputation. Offer him a hundred and see what he tells you."

"How do I get in touch with him?"

"He'll probably get in touch with you."

"What if he doesn't?"

"Look him up in the phone book," Lord said.

CHAPTER THREE

Andy Fannell, once termed "the Bugsy Siegal of the East" by a zealous congressman, held court at his roadhouse, the Holiday Inn, three times a week, much as a benign block-leader politician might do. The morning after Judge Yorty was shot, Fannell listened to a friend of his who had a friend who worked as a warehouse loader in town. The loader was in bad shape; his wife needed surgery; the shylocks on the loading platform were into him; he could not pay them, and they had roughed him up pretty good.

"If he gets a chance he'll pay what he owes, Andy," the loader's friend told Fannell. And Fannell brought his fingers tentlike to his lips and said, "Who's the shylock?"

"Guy named Thiaux. He's number one."

"Ask him if he can't drop by to talk about it."

The other man made a phone call to see if the moneylending platform man named Thiaux couldn't spare a few minutes to drop out and see Andy Fannell.

Thiaux was there inside of an hour.

"Sit down," Fannell said to him, and Thiaux sat down. Fannell seemed moody, but came at once to the point. "Lend to a man named Hazlitt?"

"That bastard," Thiaux said.

"You work with the foreman, don't you?"

Thiaux nodded.

"You see Hazlitt's pay envelope before he does?"

Thiaux moistened his lips and nodded again. It still was winter, but he felt uncommonly warm sitting here.

"How much you been holding out?"

"Forty dollars," Thiaux said.

"That's too much."

"He got himself borrowing," Thiaux said defensively. "I didn't tell him to borrow."

"You're the only one he could have borrowed from." It was a statement, not a question.

"All right, but so?" Thiaux said. "You borrow, you ought to pay back."

"He'll pay it back," Fannell said. "He's got trouble at home. Bills. From now on you hold out fifteen dollars a week from his pay envelope."

Thiaux sighed.

"Don't belt him around any more either," Fannell said.

"All right," Thiaux said. Then, a justifying afterthought occurred. "He told me he was going to the cops if I didn't let him alone."

"Nobody ever goes to the cops," Fannell said, and the way he said it, it was a threat and a promise and a simple declaration, all at the same time.

And it was the truth. No warehouse loader in Andy Fannell's territory ever took his troubles to the police. The police could not do anything. The police would not do anything.

The law, for the men in the loading locals, came instead from the man who would and could enforce the law—Andy Fannell, racketeer czar of the warehouse and building trades.

And who would say justice was served the less? Not, certainly, that good-souled, law-abiding citizen John Hazlitt, the loader who had borrowed too much money from Thiaux, the platform shylock. Fannell's justice protected John Hazlitt to the point where now he could go to his wife's bedside in the hospital and weep in front of her because some man he did not know—he would not know Fannell if he saw him—had said the words that now protected his money and his job and his body. Had John Hazlitt threatened to go to the police? Maybe that was what he had told Thiaux, maybe those were the words that came from his lips, but nothing could have been farther from his actual thoughts. Indeed, there was a special irony here, for John Hazlitt had a younger brother who was a policeman—a foot patrolman in Aimerly. And he had told his brother nothing.

For that matter, Alf Hazlitt, the loader's brother, had his own troubles. This same day, the day after the judge died, he stood watch outside in the hall when four men from police headquarters raided an apartment in the center of Aimerly city. There were voices from inside the apartment, and after a time the four headquarters men came out, and with them were two other men. One of the police said to Alf Hazlitt, "Stay here. We're going down the street to talk to some people."

And they disappeared, and Alf Hazlitt stood there, young and new in his policeman's uniform; but after a time, assuring himself all the while it was being done in the course of duty, he opened the door to the apartment and looked in.

At first, what he saw did not register. To the right, and just under the casement window of the large room in which he stood, was a large telephone switchboard, complete with jacks, toggles, and headsets. Against the far wall, five tape recorders sat side by side on the floor; four of the five were closed, but the fifth still had the cover up, the tape wide and thick on the ready spool. While closed, the other recorders in their suitcase-type equipment were not locked; two of the headsets hung by their wire alongside the switchboard panel, and the jacks lay in wiry, rubbery disarray at the base of the switchboard as if they had been pulled all too hurriedly from their connections.

They might as well have been left in place, though. For alongside the several female contacts on the board there were little slips of paper, such as the kind that are placed in the name-plate apertures of apartment mail boxes. And for no reason that he knew, Alf Hazlitt took out his notebook and wrote down what it said on each of the slips.

What it said was:

> MAin 3-6139   PRospect 4-8794
> PRospect 4-8788 MAin 3-0062
> PRospect 4-8790 MAin 3-0068

Then he went back to his post, outside in the hall.

CHAPTER FOUR

B Y THE CALENDAR, IT WAS LATE WINTER ... THE LAST week of winter. One week later, also by the calendar, it was spring. All in that time, however, the weather had not changed. It was the weather of false spring, false in all respects, so that no one had a good word for it. Everyone knew that this far north the cold would come again, would stay through April, would beat, finally, a slow, bushwhacking retreat. Now, all that the warm weather did was to up the number of head colds in town, overheat one or two automobiles, and cause Ben Phillips, running for the Board of Aldermen, to campaign coatless and hatless. He showed up that way on Rain Street in Aimerly at four o'clock of a Tuesday afternoon. "Boys," he said, "I'm going to talk about this town. I'm going to roll up my sleeves and talk. You know where I'm going to do my talking? Right on the hotel porch. Right where the old judge died." A little thing it was—brave, symbolic, but a little thing. Ben Phillips strode out onto the porch of the Kamm Hotel in his shirt sleeves that afternoon, and had a crowd there waiting for him—not too big a crowd, but a curious one.

They didn't even send a lieutenant to stop him. They sent a patrolman instead. He asked Ben Phillips if there was a permit to hold a public meeting.

"I got no permit," Ben said.

"Can't hold no meeting, then," the cop said.

"They didn't have no permit when they shot down the judge," Ben said.

"He wasn't holding no meeting," the cop said.

"You must feel proud, working for a town like this."

"You're the one's running for office," the cop said. "Not me."

But that was where the crowd was, in front of the Kamm Hotel on Rain Street, and nowhere else, and the town was of a size—45,000 in Aimerly proper—that when its available daytime idlers gathered in one place, then other places would take on a look unpeopled and bereft.

That was the look the depot had about it when the local got in at 4:13 p.m. from Port Gerard. The train was on time. It was always on time, even in a period of heavy snows, because the timetable afforded a spectacular margin for error. There was margin allowed even for the two per cent grade climbing for a mile and a half out of Port Gerard.

Sam Murray got off the local. He looked around the station and saw no one, and for a small space in time he said to himself the thing to do was get back on the train and the hell with all things. But he shook his head. "No," he said, talking aloud to himself. "Here you are and here you stay. Sam, you're a good man. Give you plenty loving—treat you right—because a good man nowadays is hard to find." He hoisted his bag, and then he said to himself, aloud again, "What loving?"

He told the cab driver to take him to the office of the *Times*, and to drop his luggage off at the Kamm Hotel. The driver thought that was funny. He said, "The Kamm's on the way to the *Times*."

"Do it the way I said anyway, will you please?" Murray said. "Take me to the paper and then leave the stuff off. Is that all right?"

"Sure it's all right," the driver said. He turned at an intersection that had an old-fashioned police pagoda in the center, with a white-gloved policeman, covered by an umbrella, directing traffic; and they started up Rain Street. The driver said, "That's the hotel right there."

"That where they shoot the judge?"

"Like a scared she-deer in season," the driver said.

"Don't say," Sam Murray said, and he did not look further, but sat back in the rear seat until the driver stopped the cab. Then Murray looked out the window, and there was irritation in his voice. "I said the *Times* building."

"This here is where it's at," the driver said.

"This is a bank building."

The driver nodded. "How damn fool you want to get? It's a building with a bank in it and the paper in it, too. You think you got a separate building for everything in this town? Even the morgue where they took the old judge, they had a dice game going on downstairs."

Murray reached for his wallet. "Would you say that made this town sinful or just overcrowded?"

"I wouldn't say," the driver said.

"Keep the change," Murray said.

"Except," the driver said, "nobody ever has to stand up on the bus."

Murray got out of the cab and found that the office of the *Times* was on the second floor of the bank building; the newsroom was on the third floor. Sam decided he would try the office on the second floor. It did not look anything like a newspaper office, but on the other hand you could make a case for saying this town did not look like a town. Murray went inside, and there was an old man, a thin old man with a bright-blue vest and an eyeshade, sitting at a desk back of a partition that consisted of a row of olive-green filing cabinets stacked shoulder-high. Sam Murray rapped with his knuckles on the top of the cabinets; it made a hollow, sound-effects kind of noise. The old man looked up and Sam said, "I wanted to see himself."

"I'm himself."

"The one inside."

"Ayuh."

"I'm Murray from Port Gerard. Crime commission. I'm looking for Leclerc."

"I'm Leclerc," the old man said. He had not moved from his desk, though from what Sam Murray could see there was nothing on the desk to keep him busy.

"Don't look at me like I ought to act more excited," the old man named Leclerc said. "Go through that door over there and I'll meet you inside."

Murray went through the door, and there was a little hallway beyond, and after that a small, square room with another desk, and by the time Sam got there the old man was there, too, coming in by the side door.

"Sit down," Leclerc said. He had the clean-dirty look of old men who go too long without shaving. When Murray had seated himself, the old man did likewise, and produced a cigarette holder of extraordinary length. He said, "What are you smoking?"

"I'm not," Murray said.

"Drink?"

"All right."

"Gin this early?"

"Bourbon if you've got it."

"Mind a paper cup?"

"Put one paper cup inside another one," Sam Murray said, and the old man got up and went to the old-fashioned water cooler in the corner of the room next to the window. He opened the ice compartment and drew out two bottles. One was a bottle of gin.

"Four Roses," Leclerc said, staring at the other bottle and holding it up the way an obstetrician holds up a baby upon delivery.

"Use the extra paper cup," Murray said. "Otherwise it eats through."

"If you drink slow," Leclerc said.

"I don't like to worry about it one way or the other."

Leclerc shrugged and thrust one conical paper cup within another and poured in the whisky and handed it across the desk to Murray. Then, doing it thoughtfully, he gazed at the bottle of gin in the cooler, looked at the bottle in his hand, and poured himself a drink of Four Roses, using a single cup.

"So," Leclerc said, and sat down again. "He drinks but he doesn't smoke. Let's see, now. What else?" A thought occurred to him. "Bring a gun?"

"Nope."

The old man put his feet up on the desk. "I always thought," he said, "that carrying a gun was the greatest excuse in the world for getting shot. The other man can always claim self-defense."

"A good philosophy," Murray said.

"On the other hand," Leclerc said, "old Judge Yorty didn't carry a gun. And they still shot him."

"But not in self-defense," Murray said.

"Who knows?" Leclerc said. "Who knows?"

"When did they shoot him?"

"Week ago today."

"Anything happen since?"

"Police chief's daughter got married."

"Anything else?"

"Nope. That's why you're here, hey?"

"Not me," Murray said.

"I'll bet," Leclerc said.

Murray shook his head. "You lose. I don't want to know who killed the judge."

"No?"

"No."

"Who does if you don't?"

"Beats me," Sam said. "Maybe you."

"Why me?"

"You're a newspaper."

"Crusade department four doors down," Leclerc said shortly. "All we're interested in is better sewers."

Sam Murray put his right hand to his left ear lobe and rubbed there with his thumb. It was a characteristic gesture. "Look," he said, "I'm from a crime commission. What are crime commissions in business for?"

"I'll bite," Leclerc said. "Are you going to give me the bit about the white-hot light of public attention, focused on wrongdoing?"

"Cynic," Murray said. "My, my."

"Cynic is right," Leclerc said. "My paper does not desire the Pulitzer Prize. My television station does not desire the Peabody Award."

"But you desire circulation," Murray said to him. "Don't you agree?"

"Does that drink need touching?" Leclerc said, and reached with the hand that held the cigarette holder, until he saw that Murray still had some whisky left. The old man leaned again and stared at his visitor. "So? You already said you weren't interested in who killed the judge."

"I'm not. I'm interested in newspaper space. It's what the crime commission does for a living. Raise enough hell in public—that means the newspapers, TV, radio, magazines, so forth—and maybe you get action. Action you wouldn't get otherwise."

"Action from this town?" Leclerc snorted audibly.

"No," Murray said. "From the state legislature."

"Oh-ho," the publisher said. "New state law. Make murder illegal."

"Not murder."

"Not murder?"

"No. Wiretapping."

"What?"

"You've heard of it," Murray said.

"Yeah. But what's the judge dying got to do with it?"

"Because," Sam said, and took his hand away from his ear, "that's the way newspapers work."

"You know a lot about newspapers."

"Yes, yes," Sam said to him. "You know what I am? An animal in a vegetable kingdom. Know why I'm honest? Because there's nothing left by the time they get to me. If you can fix the judge and the D.A. and the cop on the beat, why mess with the slob from the crime commission? He can't hurt you anyway."

"But you're here in town. You come because they murdered the judge, but you're not interested in the murder. You're interested in wiretapping. You'd better have another drink. Just on general principles."

"Maybe I will," Sam said. "Here. I'll get it." He stood up, lanky and hard-boned, and went and refilled his drink. "You know Joe Thomas?"

"The county prosecutor?" Leclerc nodded. "Well?"

"Thomas does a lot of wiretap work."

"Maybe he does. It's legal in this state. If you get a court order."

"Righto," Sam Murray said. He sat down again. "You know, prosecutors are only human, like the rest of us. Every one of them's got his own particular favorite judge or two. Now, in the case of Joe Thomas, there was only one judge who'd sign any tap order Joe brought in. Not only police taps. Thomas has a private law practice on the side. Maybe he's had a client or two who could use the same service. So Joe had himself a judge—Judge Yorty—the one somebody shot last week."

Leclerc leaned back and stroked at his stubble of beard. "Joe Thomas has all kinds of trouble, I'd say. There's a liquor-store fellow named Ben Phillips running for alderman against Joe Thomas's man. Phillips and Thomas don't get along at all."

"I'm not interested in elections, either," Murray said. "All I'm telling you is you may hear from me on the wiretap thing. If I can uncover anything."

"Think you can?"

Murray shrugged. "I got two things going for me. One is money. I can pay for information."

"Want me to put a notice in the paper? 'Mr. Murray of the crime commission is here. Money for information about wiretapping so he can make a big hit with the state legislature.' Something like that?"

"If you'd like to," Murray said amiably. "I got something else going for me, too. Justice, or whatever the hell you call it. The constitution. Fourth amendment. Privacy of the individual—unreasonable search—so forth."

"If you had enough justice, you wouldn't need the money," Leclerc said.

"I'm glad you put it that way," Sam Murray said. "For a minute I was afraid you were a real pessimist. I thought you were going to say if I had enough money, I wouldn't need the justice."

CHAPTER FIVE

Joe Thomas, district attorney for Aimerly County, regretted the death—not so much the death of Judge Yorty as the death of his own chief investigator, Steve Yaros, who had died of nothing more suspicious than hardened arteries some three months before. Yaros was Joe Thomas's bag man. There was no other way to describe it. Yaros was the man who knew the men Joe Thomas ought not to know. He was the enforcer, though he never had to enforce. The county tolerated gambling, even if the law did not, and the thin line in between was the one where Steve Yaros danced, hands spread like a tightrope walker, palms of hands conveniently cupped in case you wanted to put money there. With Steve Yaros at his side, Joe Thomas had paid off the mortgage on his farm within two years of becoming county prosecutor. Indeed, Thomas maintained a private practice now not only for the income but really in spite of it. It was well known that a mid-state county prosecutor did not earn enough in salary as district attorney to live the way Joe Thomas lived, so Joe Thomas could always point to his private law practice as the source of his added income.

Now Yaros was dead, and Joe Thomas had decided the smart thing to do was to ride out the forthcoming local election before deciding upon a new chief investigator. Though the prosecutor was not himself up for re-election, he was answerable to the Aimerly City Board of Aldermen. It was an off-year, even locally speaking, and only one aldermanic post was being contested.

If it was won by Joe Thomas's man, a man named Wenninger, things would be all right; but if the rival candidate, Ben Phillips, won, then care would be in order, for the majority on the board depended on the seat in contest.

And Ben Phillips was going around town yapping about crime in general and poor Judge Yorty in particular. Vaguely, Joe Thomas wished something would happen to get Judge Yorty off page one of the paper. He had even had Police Chief Halverson move up the date of his daughter's wedding, just to provide a different kind of local news, but nothing had worked. The wedding, in fact, had backfired, because Halverson had happily taken off for Port Gerard, where the wedding was to take place, and thus could not supply the answers Joe Thomas needed on a subject newly at hand.

It was a copy of a routine police-raid report, written in laborious police-academy English by the detective in charge of the raid. It described how an informant, one of several police links at the telephone company, had tipped the location of a wiretap nest. Upon raiding the apartment, the report went on, the detectives found equipment described as follows .... plus two men, one of whom identified himself as Felix Morton, a telephone company employee, who said he had done several similar jobs for Captain Macy of the Confidential Squad, Aimerly Police Department, and implied that the present set-up was a similar assignment. Detectives concluded therefore that the perpetrators were on official business. Thus the equipment was left untouched and no arrests made. At the time of the raid, the listening post had recorders tapping the following numbers: Main 3-6139, 0062, and 0068; Prospect 4-8788, 8790, and 8794.

What Police Chief Halverson might have to say about this, when he got back from his daughter's wedding, was something

Joe Thomas was excessively eager to hear. No news of the raid had leaked to the public; for this Thomas was grateful.

Thomas had been toying for a time with the notion of having a private little talk with Ben Phillips. Thomas was a very powerful man. He had the one weapon that is the most forceful weapon in all of law—a grand jury. At his whim and fancy, any district attorney can call a man to give testimony before a grand jury, regardless of whether that man has committed a crime or is even suspected of one. And regardless of whether the grand jury hands down or even considers an indictment, the very presence of a man as a grand jury witness often, in the appearances of things, could work against him. Thomas, sitting in his office now, had been contemplating a most outrageous device—to call Ben Phillips before the grand jury and ask him questions about Judge Yorty. The inference would be that Phillips had something to do with the judge's death—perhaps he even wanted him dead, so as to provide himself with a campaign issue ("A great judge, shot down like a dog in the streets, etc., etc.").

But Thomas's urge to get Phillips on the phone now was defeated by two other considerations. One was that such a bald stunt as the one he contemplated, dragging Phillips in front of the jury, could be dangerous—could backfire.

And, staring at his phone, Joe Thomas thought of the other reason, too. For the first time as a serious consideration, it occurred to the district attorney, who had tapped or ordered the tapping of five thousand phones in his prosecutor's lifetime, that somebody might be listening to *him*.

CHAPTER SIX

IT WAS AFTER SUPPER, AND ALF HAZLITT, THE POLICEMAN who had been stationed outside in the hall when the raid occurred on the tap nest, surveyed the nightly ruins. Two small preschool children, more than enough despite some hazy high school promise Alf had made himself to father a family of eight, had finally been put to bed for the night. Evidence of their good health and well-being was everywhere. Half of a plastic trailer truck showed from beneath a sofa ruffle—just enough of it visible, in fact, to assure Alf and his wife Anne that the other half was missing and must be the object of an all-night search. Alf stooped over tiredly and picked up one candy-striped sock. Its mate, for all he knew, might be stuffed inside the missing half of the truck. To the side of the arm chair lay, half buried in the carpet, three marbles, placed in diabolical tangency so that a father was bound to slip on one of them and break his leg.

Anne was in the kitchen, which itself managed to look, after supper in this family, like a bivouac for the National Guard. She came to the door of the kitchen, dish towel in one hand and sudsy saucepan in the other, and looked out at her husband.

"That's it," she said, mad without being really mad, "the slow motion kid."

Alf straightened up. Well. Four and a half years of marriage. And he had no stomach for the fight, and did not wish to make an issue over the rate of speed at which he was willing to pick objects up off the floor. All he said was, "I wish I had a hundred thousand dollars."

But Anne was back in the kitchen with the water running, and did not hear him. Men, she knew, had their own problems, and you had to pick your spots with them, and seek the right openings for whatever you wanted to tell them, and oftentimes be gentle with them when they came home from work.

When finally she emerged from the kitchen, undoing her apron, she found Alf in the armchair, cheek propped on hand. "There it is," he said, and indicated a fairly respectable-looking pile of juvenile miscellany. "Found the other sock. The one for the left foot."

Anne sank onto the couch and pulled her legs up under her. He looked at her and said to himself, as he said to himself often but did not say so often to her, that this was one lalapalooza of a wife. She said, "How did you know it was for the left foot?"

"Because the hole is where the right big toe is," Bill said, "so they'll wear longer if the kid changes feet."

Anne smiled, but her eyes were taking inventory. "Where's the other half of the truck?"

"Ah," Alf said, "Inspector Lestrade of Scotland Yard. Captain Macy of the Confidential Squad. Where is the other half of the truck, indeed?"

"Did you look in the drawer of your desk?"

"No."

"Why not?"

Alf studied for a moment. "I don't think I know why not."

"Try it and see," Anne said.

"In your all-pervading wisdom," he said to her, "I'm positive that the drawer of my desk is where the missing half of the truck is, so let's leave it there for half a mo. The old man's bushed."

"Me too," Anne said, and looked at him carefully. "What was it you said when I was in the kitchen?"

Alf thought. "Oh," he said, "I know. I said I wished I had a hundred thousand dollars."

Anne brightened. "That's fun."

"Ah, yes," he said. "A hundred thousand. Big ones."

"A hundred thousand dollars," she said.

"After taxes," Alf said, and yawned luxuriously.

"What would we do with it?"

"We?"

"Oh," Anne said. "I'm sorry. I forgot. It's your money."

"Damn right," he said:

"Well," she said. "Then what would *you* do with it?"

He pursed his lips and began to nod, speculatively. "Offhand, I don't know what I'd do with all that money. But after all, how important is that?"

Anne shook her head. "I don't follow."

"I mean," he said, "you can always *do* something with that money." He cocked an index finger. "The big thing is get ahold of it."

"Yes," Anne said. "I can see it's a matter of planning."

"Everything must be doped out in advance," Alf said. "If I have a hundred thousand dollars, am I in this little development house slipping on marbles and breaking my spine? I ask you. Am I? Am I a cop for a living?"

"No," Anne said.

"Right, wife," he said, and became bemused with this and tried to say *right wife* three times, fast, and could not do it.

"Let me," Anne said, and she tried, and came up at once with *rate rife.*

"Wight rife," Alf said.

"Ladies," Anne said, "have you tried the new washday miracle, Wight Rife?"

"Let science take over your laundry chores," Alf said. "No more blue Mondays, for Wight Rife contains the new wonder ingredient, DL-44."

"No other soap can make that statement," Anne said.

"Perhaps I should telephone Herb across the street and tell him of our discovery," Alf said, and stood up.

"On your way back," Anne said, "you can check your desk drawer for the other half of the truck."

Alf went into their bedroom, where the phone was, and back in the living room Anne realized too late that she should not have let him do this. She wanted to tell him herself, but when she came back from the doctor this afternoon she had told Doris that she was pregnant again, and Doris undoubtedly had told Herb and now Herb would say something to Alf about it over the phone.

That was the way it happened. Curiously, Alf Hazlitt was not unduly angry over the fact that Anne had not told him at once. More fundamentally, he thought of the irony in wanting a hundred thousand dollars. A hundred dollars would be more like it. Where, he wondered, would they put the new baby? Where was the money for the doctor going to come from?

Hanging up the phone, he reached into his desk drawer to see if the missing half of the toy truck was there. It was not there. What was there, though, was the slip of paper on which he had written the phone numbers from the tap raid of nearly a week ago. Nothing had been said about it since—not at the precinct house, not in the newspaper or over the air. It was as if the raid had never taken place, and Alf Hazlitt, an honest cop and therefore by definition dumb, but not that dumb, had said nothing about it. To ask the lieutenant would have been to invite a rip on his record.

Still, the phone numbers were here.

A hundred thousand dollars.

No, a hundred dollars.

Alf Hazlitt went back into the living room, to stage mock anger against his wife for not having told him at once about the baby.

CHAPTER SEVEN

S AM MURRAY WALKED THE FOUR BLOCKS FROM THE NEWS-paper to the Kamm Hotel. They told him at the hotel desk that his bags already had been sent upstairs, but there was a phone message for him—a number for him to call—so he stopped first at the pay phone in the lobby.

A man's voice answered the phone.

"Sam Murray," Sam said. "Who's this?"

"Millburn."

"Harry Millburn?"

"That's right," the voice said. "They tell you about me in Port Gerard?"

"I know about you," Sam said. And it was true. Millburn's reputation was wide. He was a private detective. He was an acknowledged expert in the frightening science of electronics. The two capacities, in combination, made him a man to reckon with. Murray could quote from memory the memo he had brought with him from Walter Lord, managing director of the state anti-crime commission: *Have arranged for private detective, also tap expert, name of Harry Millburn, get in touch with you.* Millburn was losing no time. Sam Murray said into the phone, "You know what I'm here for?"

"Yup."

"We want to start something moving with the legislature on the wiretapping situation," Murray said. "It's out of hand."

"Well, Goody Two-Shoes," Millburn said.

"Don't be any sweeter than you have to," Murray said into the phone. "I want to see you."

"Where you calling from?"

"Hotel. Pay booth."

"I'm in a booth, too. Been waiting around downstairs for an hour, until you called."

"What's the matter with upstairs?"

"The apartment?" Millburn laughed a short, unpleasant laugh. "My phone's a party line."

"Who's listening?"

"Three cops. Want their names?"

"What'd you do wrong?"

"Nothing. They wanted some money and I said no. I've got seventy-five thousand dollars' worth of tap equipment in my place. Half of it you can't find anywhere else. I got a license and a lawyer so it'd be easier for them to shake me down than to try to seize the stuff. Therefore they listen. Also look. There's one of them in a Chevrolet parked across the street right now."

"Can you meet me?"

"I'd like to shake the plain-clothes first."

"Want me to get rid of him for you?"

"He's pretty good. I think he must have gone to Carnegie Tech."

"What color is the car?"

"Black. Two-door."

"What's the address?"

"Elm Street, corner of Norcross Way."

"What's a good restaurant?"

"The place in the hotel is good."

"Stay there for five minutes," Sam Murray said. "Then walk out of there and meet me here. Nobody'll follow you."

"Whoopsee doo," the voice named Harry Millburn said sarcastically. "What's the password?"

"Goody Two-Shoes," Murray said, and hung up the phone. He saw that the local directory was hanging on a chain inside the booth. On the cover, it said:

IN CASE OF EMERGENCY
FIRE—MAin 3-4040
POLICE—MAin 3-2000

Murray called the police first. "Listen," he said to the desk man who answered, "inside of ten minutes a bomb's going to go off from inside a black Chevrolet. Elm Street and Norcross Way. You hear me?"

"Elm Street and Norcross Way," the voice said; then did a take. "What?"

"A bomb," Sam said, and hung up the phone. He grinned for a moment and rubbed his ear lobe, then dropped another dime in and dialed the fire department. "Fire in an automobile," he said. "Black Chevrolet. Elm Street and Norcross Way."

"Right!" It was the voice of a 110% fireman. "Don't leave the scene."

Murray grinned again and went across the lobby of the hotel and into the restaurant. He was the only customer at this time of day, and he went and stood at the bar and decided he would stick with Four Roses. He said to the bartender, "Got an election coming up?"

The bartender was filling his ice compartment. He said, "Nah. Couple of aldermen."

"Doesn't mean anything?"

"Somebody wins, somebody loses," the bartender said. "My bookie stays in business."

"Why do you bother to vote?"

"Who said I do?"

Sam nodded and went back to his drink. After a time he looked up and saw that a man and a woman had come into the dining room. The man was short and chubby, with a seraphic face—all of it hut the eyes, which were too small and set a little too close together. He was, Murray judged, about forty years of age, and he had blond hair that was almost white.

The girl with him was better to look at; any girl would have been better to look at, but this one was extremely so. She too was blond, but her figure was unusually good. She wore a dress that was too summery for this time of year, but on her it looked fine. Her legs were long and silken, and she had the kind of walk that made a man who watched her from in front want to watch her from behind.

The newcomers came over to the bar, the man looking searchingly at Murray.

"Murray?" he said. "Sam Murray?"

Murray nodded.

"Harry Millburn," the man said, and stuck out his hand. "My sister Ellie."

Sam shook hands, looking into the girl's eyes. He said. "Let's get a table."

"I'll order for us," Millburn said, and Murray and Ellie Millburn went and sat at a table along the wall halfway between the bar and the doorway that led from the dining room to the hotel lobby. Sam said to Ellie, "Were you with your brother when I talked to him on the phone?"

She nodded. "It was my day off."

"From what?"

She paused, as though she was not accustomed to the direct question. Then she said, "I work for the paper."

"Doing what?"

"Society," the girl said. "Home hints. Degree in journalism from the University of Missouri."

Sam looked at her. Then said, "Anybody follow you?"

Ellie laughed; she laughed as though she were not quite sure it was the thing to do, but the sound of her laughter startled him nonetheless and made him newly aware. She said, "Let Harry tell you."

Millburn came over and sat down. He had whisky for himself and a wine for Ellie. Sam said to him, "Goody Two-Shoes."

"Never mind," Millburn said. He stirred his drink. "You're all right, buddy. You pass."

"Trouble?"

"Not for me. That poor plain-clothes in the car never saw so many fire engines and cops in his life. They hit him like a ton of bricks. By the time anybody made any sense out of anything, we were three blocks away."

"What's the story?"

Millburn shrugged. "Tapping's a funny business. It's my business."

"That makes you a real specialist?"

"Pretty much so. I'm the only fellow in town who's got all three requirements—the training, the equipment, *and* the private detective's license. So the work comes to me."

"The illegal work."

"Legal work," Millburn said. "It doesn't have to be dishonest just because it's not done on court order." His voice had an intense lecturing quality. "This happens to be one of thirty-two states where it's legal for a man to tap his own phone. Let's say I suspect my wife of running around. Who do I go to? The police? Don't be silly. I go to a private detective. Or I go to a lawyer and *he* goes to a private detective. I say I want my phone tapped—so I can listen in on my wife."

The girl, Ellie, said, "And it's admissible in court?"

It was Sam Murray's turn. "Oh, hell, yes," he said. "And more than that. Suppose I'm up for murder. I plead not guilty and then I go home and talk to my lawyer on the phone and make some admission to him. They've tapped my phone. They can take that recording and play it in court and have it admitted as evidence, under the law of this state, and New York, and a couple of dozen others, even though they openly violated the privileged nature of a lawyer-client relationship. They can do it with doctor and patient, husband and wife, priest and penitent."

"Wahoo," Harry Millburn said.

Murray nodded. "I guess it sounds pretty schmaltzy."

"Where'd you read it out of?"

"Here and there."

"Well, you missed the big kicker," Millburn said. "It doesn't have to be just a husband who's worried about his wife. It can be an insurance company trying to check up on claims or an industrialist who suspects one of his subordinates or something like that." He gestured with his hand. "But let's say it's a husband and wife. I have my phone tapped because I suspect my wife. Some way or other she suspects it and she goes to the police and says, 'I think my phone's being tapped.' The cops check it out. Now what do they do? They can confirm that it's being tapped, even though the husband has given his written permission to have it done to his own phone, so it's legal. Then maybe they seize the equipment and the poor private detective who leased the stuff out in the first place has to sue them to get it back. Or they go to the husband and the private detective and say, 'Look, we know what you're doing. We also know it's legal. We also know if we tell the wife there *is* a tap, it'll ruin what you're trying to do. So how about it?' And you've got no choice but to pay the cops off. You might say that's the number one reason they're sore at me around here. A couple of times they asked me if I wanted to pay and I told them where to go."

"Nice cops around here," Murray said.

"Nice cops around anywhere," Millburn said.

"No," Murray said. "I know some good bulls."

"I don't."

"Most cops are honest."

"All cops are human. They start at thirty-four hundred a year. They've got to deal with graft and protection and the slob on the highway who wants to give them ten to forget the ticket. Ten dollars. That's forty quarts of Grade-A milk for the cop's kids at home. What do you want from a cop's life?"

Sam Murray could not escape the feeling that Harry Millburn's eyes were set too close together. It was an unreasonable feeling, an unjustifiable opinion, but still it was there. He said aloud, "What are you talking to me for?"

Harry Millburn looked at him archly. "Why," he said, "the word is out. Didn't you know?"

Sam Murray looked at Millburn, then at his watching sister, then back again. Any way you cut it, he liked the sister better. He said, "Walter Lord told me to get in touch with you."

"See?" Millburn said. "Nothing I like better to do than help you crime commission fellows."

"Come on," Murray said.

"Well," Millburn said, "put it this way. I don't get along with the police. I don't get along with the phone company. I—"

Murray said, "The phone company?"

"The phone company," Millburn said. "You do legal tap work, whether police or not, you're liable to run into them. If it's legal, then the phone company gets a copy of any court order a judge signs to tap a line. If a lawyer does it for a client, then probably he's got a phone company employee helping out. You know. The actual tap. So forth."

"All right," Murray said. "So. You don't get along with the police. You don't get along with the phone company. Who else don't you get along with?"

"Andy Fannell," Millburn said.

"Big labor racketeer," Murray said. "Well. Runs this county. Anybody else?"

"Joe Thomas."

"The county prosecutor," Murray said. "Delightful. The police, the D.A., the phone company, and the fellow from the underworld. You know what I think?"

"No," Millburn said. He finished his drink. "What do you think?"

"I think this is fine talk."

"Meaning?"

"Meaning you haven't told me a damn thing."

"No?"

"No."

"Look, dad," Harry Millburn said, "doesn't it occur to you I'm taking a chance even showing up where you are?"

"Only if I believe your game of cops and robbers," Murray said.

"Don't you?"

"I don't know. It's different than the kind I used to play. The way I always played it, I got to hide my eyes and count to a hundred by fives."

"Speaking of fives," Millburn said.

"All right," Murray said. "Fifty dollars."

"Not enough," Millburn said.

"What do you want?"

"Two hundred."

"I'll give you fifty now and fifty later. If anything comes of it."

"You can go to hell," Millburn said smoothly.

"What can you do?"

"I can take you to a place the cops raided last week. A wiretap nest. What do you think of that?"

"It's worth a hundred dollars to the anti-crime commission," Sam Murray said.

"A hundred and a quarter," Millburn said.

Murray looked at him. "You starve for that twenty-five, don't you?"

"Waste not, want not," Harry Millburn said. "It ain't your money. You're supposed to pay for information."

"All right," Sam Murray said. He looked at the girl, but her face told him nothing.

"And afterward," Millburn said, "why don't you ask Ellie out to supper?"

"I might," Murray said. He reached for his wallet and smiled at the girl. "How would that strike you?"

"Perfect," she said.

"No checks," Harry Millburn said, watching Sam Murray's wallet. "I'm an amateur."

CHAPTER EIGHT

E VERYBODY LISTENED TO THE 7:30 NEWS TELECAST OVER WACX-TV. Everybody in Aimerly waited for Bill Voss, the announcer, to get through with his boresome national and international headlines and say, "… And now for the local news."

Tonight the local news was something special. For old Leclerc, the publisher of the Aimerly *Times* and owner of the television station, had heard from Sam Murray, who earlier had been taken to the raided apartment by Harry Millburn.

Millburn, in fact, had a key to the apartment, and it interested Murray. He said to Millburn, "Your flat?"

"Nope," Millburn said.

"Where'd you get the key?"

"You ask a lot of questions, Goody."

The equipment was still in the apartment, just as it had been when the police raided the place. Murray looked around the room and said, "Looks like somebody left in a hurry."

"Somebody did," Millburn said.

"Cops walk in?"

"Not exactly. They knocked first."

"Same thing they had in New York," Sam Murray said. He scratched his ear and looked around. "Tap nest. That's what the papers called it."

"Better than New York," Harry Millburn said. "All they had there was half a dozen exchanges."

"How many here?"

"Two. But that means half the city and the whole surrounding area. They went over to dial phones last year. Two exchanges. Main 3, Prospect 4. That takes in the race track out of town and Andy Fannell's Holiday Inn. I don't have to tell you about Fannell."

He pushed the casement window open and reached out a hand. "Steel cross-box outside the window. Down the building and onto the spare pairs in the nearest telephone cable. Phone exchange building three doors away. Very nice."

Murray said, "You mean they could tap any phone on Main or Prospect?"

"Nearly twenty thousand phones," Millburn said.

"They must have had their own separate cable."

"Didn't need it. The principle's the same. For instance, the FBI does some tapping, they'll lease their own phone cable from the telephone company. That way they can listen in on as many numbers as they want from one central listening post—like this one here. But these boys didn't have to do that. Every phone company cable carries spare wires. In the big cities, one cable might carry twenty-one hundred wires. But only fifteen hundred will be in actual use. Same with this one here. They moved in on the spare pairs. Then the connection's made on the main frame in the phone building and—"

"Wait a minute," Sam Murray said. "Who does that?"

"Guys who work for the phone company," Millburn said patiently. "Who did you think?"

"You mean there were phone company employees in on this?"

Millburn nodded. "I don't think there are any more. The phone company doesn't like that kind of thing. If it comes to their attention, that is."

"I thought you said the police already raided this place."

"They did."

"Who'd they arrest?"

"Nobody."

"Why not?"

"Oh, stop it," Millburn said to him. "Who are they going to arrest? The cops did their sworn duty. They said, "Look, no more wiretapping around here, 'cause mamma don' want.'"

"Who's mamma?"

"If you knew that, you'd know why there were no arrests."

"Do you know it?"

"Not me," Harry Millburn said. He flipped his cigarette against the suitcase handle of one of the tape recorders, and it fell, still aglow, to the floor.

Sam Murray said to him, "How do you know anything about this?"

Millburn grinned. "I got friends."

"Where?"

"Phone company. Among other places. I'll tell you a funny thing. When the cops got the tip on this place, the tip was they were going to find *me* here! By now, you've got the idea they don't like me. So here they came—and it wasn't me at all. Imagine! Some other team. The Boston Red Sox or somebody, but not little old Harry. Ah. The plot thickens. The police are confused." He spat on the floor, and Ellie Millburn said, "Harry!"

"All right," Sam Murray said. "Next question. What phones were they listening to?"

"How do I know?" Millburn said. "I told you they could listen to any phone they wanted to. That's what the switchboard's here for."

Ellie said, "But how did they know when somebody was talking on whatever particular line they were interested in? I mean, if they weren't just listening in on one given phone, how could they tell? Did something light up?"

"The recorders," Millburn said. "They're actuated by the phone being picked up off the hook." He looked down at the recording equipment on the floor. "Matter of fact, I'll bet they were voice-actuated. That's even better. Some people'll try to get around a tap, assuming they suspect one, by picking the phone up off the hook and leaving it there, figuring they'll use up the tape. Not these babies." He kicked one of them, almost fondly. "Look at that. Fifteen hours of tape on that wheel."

Ellie said stubbornly, "Then what were the earphones for?"

"Newspaper girl talkee too muchee," Millburn said. He grinned at Sam Murray. "Of all the businesses I got to be in to have a sister for a reporter."

"She only does women's news," Murray said.

"Me too, occasionally," Millburn said. "Private detectives mess in everything."

Ellie was persistent. "If the machines recorded the conversations automatically, why did they need headsets?"

"The switchboard comes with headsets, sweetness," her brother said. "And maybe the boys got a little bored sitting around and felt like listening in every now and again. Who knows?"

Sam Murray looked around the room. "Where's the thing?"

"What thing is that?"

"I don't know the name for it," Murray said. He gestured with his long fingers. "The thing they'd use to deaden the sound or whatever it is—you know, so you can't tell somebody's listening in on your phone."

Harry Millburn gazed at him sadly. "Goody," he said, "electronics has passed you by. They don't use anything like that. They don't have to."

"All right," Murray said, "but if I pick up my phone and I can tell it's being tapped—"

"Don't believe what you read in the papers all the time, crime-buster," Millburn said to him. He lit another cigarette. "You can't tell whether or not somebody's listening in on your phone. Period."

When they left the apartment, there were three things on Sam Murray's mind. Not necessarily in order of importance, they were to get rid of Millburn, take his sister Ellie out for the evening, and phone Leclerc at the paper.

Excessive co-operation was what he got. Harry Millburn himself duked off at the corner, saying he had a client to see and adjuring Murray to go slow with his sister. Then Ellie waited while Sam ducked into a drugstore and made the call to Leclerc.

That was how the news got on the television at 7:30.

Everybody in Aimerly watched the news on WACX-TV. Everybody included the county prosecutor and the chief of police, Andy Fannell at the Holiday Inn, Ben Phillips, who was running against the administration man for alderman, and Alf Hazlitt, the cop.

Leclerc was a canny newsman. Believe Murray though he did, he had hung the entire report squarely on Sam Murray's head.

"This information was relayed," the announcer said, winding up his story of the raided tap headquarters, "by Samuel G. Murray, assistant manager of the state anti-crime commission, who is now in Aimerly and staying at the Kamm Hotel."

That last was really unnecessary.

But it was a short cut for some people, among them Alf Hazlitt, the policeman, who knew that the anti-crime commission would pay for information and protect its sources. He did not get to meet Sam Murray until after midnight. They met in the lobby of the Kamm. And there was still time for Murray to catch the morning edition of the Aimerly *Times:*

REVEAL POLICE RAID ON CITY-WIDE
WIRETAPPING OPERATION

It was not a particularly good headline, but it told enough for a paper that did not have to reckon with any rival competition. And the story itself told it all:

A hushed-up police raid has located the headquarters of an illegal wiretapping operation that recorded conversations from at least six private telephones and could conceivably have been cut in to half the phones in the city and metropolitan area, the Times *learned last night.*

Confronted with this shocking evidence, Police Chief Martin Halverson admitted that the raid took place last Friday on an apartment at 107 Forest Street, but said no arrests were made. Chief Halverson returned yesterday from a week-end at Port Gerard, where he yesterday gave his daughter Celia in marriage to Lt. Vincent F. Clay of the Army Engineers (see elsewhere on this page for the Times *account of the wedding), and said, "I intend to get to the bottom of this at once."*

Meanwhile, the Times *also learned that the recording apparatus, which was left untouched in the apartment when police broke in to surprise two men who were supervising the tap operation, could be hooked to any number on the exchanges of MAin 3 and PRospect 4.*

First disclosure of the infamous tap nest was made by Samuel G. Murray, assistant manager of the private state anti-crime commission, who said it was the commission's purpose to bring this kind of wrongdoing to the attention of the public. Murray, who arrived here from Port Gerard yesterday, also supplied a list of six phone numbers which were being tapped by the raided headquarters.

A check by the Times disclosed that one of the numbers discovered by Murray belonged to Judith Chasen, shapely singer at the Holiday Inn.

Three others were executive office lines at the Kennedy Metals Laboratories, 35 Bank Road.

The remaining two were office numbers of Motron-Widders, stock brokers, 18 Rain Street.

Neither Miss Chasen nor any officials of the Kennedy or Motron-Widders firms could explain why anyone would want to listen to their conversations.

Benjamin E. Phillips, candidate for alderman in forthcoming local elections which will decide the balance of power on the City Board, called the disclosures a "damning indictment of crime in our town."

And the story went on from there, and Sam Murray, reading it in the paper the next morning, was pleased. at the publicity—but nonetheless would have rather seen it blown up in a big-city tabloid. A tab would have led off with the Chasen dame.

Murray thought back to his evening with Ellie Millburn. He liked dames.

But in its way, the evening he had spent with Ellie peeved him. Her brother Harry had left them alone, and they had had supper and, later, gone to the movies. But when he took her home and he tried to get a foot in the door, she had turned coy.

"I'm really not like that on the first date," she had said.

"Oh?" he'd said. "What are you like on the second?"

"I'm not immovable," she said, and smiled at him. No getting around it, she was a pretty girl. She said now, "You'll be in town tomorrow night, won't you?"

It was like every teaser he'd ever known in high school.

But he'd characterized himself as an animal in a vegetable kingdom, and animal he was.

"I'll call you," Ellie said. "At the hotel." Then she kissed him quickly and retreated, closing the door quite definitely behind her.

Then, back at the hotel, Sam had run into this young fellow—Alf Hazlitt was his name—who said he was a policeman and showed him credentials to prove it. Hazlitt wanted to talk. They went up to Sam's room, and Hazlitt said he'd heard the evening broadcast and that he had information for Sam.

"Why do you want to tell me about it?" Sam said.

"I'm not really sure," Alf Hazlitt said. "Why do most people give information to the anti-crime commission?"

"They want an extra buck or two," Sam said, "or they're friends of ours, or they're mad at somebody."

"Well, I don't know," Hazlitt said. "I don't even know what my information's worth. I don't mean worth, money. I mean worth, period."

"What is it?"

"Some phone numbers." Hazlitt told Murray about the raid.

It may have been the mood Murray was in. He looked sharply at the young policeman. "How damn fool can you get, telling me something like this?"

Hazlitt shook his head. "It's the kind of thing you want to tell somebody."

"You realize what can happen to you if they trace this information back?"

"I didn't think it through," Hazlitt said. "I figured it'd be good for you to know it."

Murray looked at him sharply. "Got a wife?"

Hazlitt nodded.

"Kids?"

"Two." The policeman moistened his lips. "Another on the way."

Sam Murray rubbed at his ear. "You know what these phone numbers are worth?"

"No."

"About twenty dollars."

"I don't want twenty dollars."

"I'm going to give you two hundred."

"I don't want two hundred."

"You'd better take it."

"Why?"

"You can use the money," Sam said.

"I'm not looking for charity," Hazlitt said.

"Oh, stop it," Murray said. "I'm buying you and you know it. I'm buying this information and anything else you run across. If you don't run across anything else, that's all right, too. Exposing this wiretap nest was worth a lot to the crime commission, potentially anyway. So you know the real reason you get two hundred? Because of my standard of values, that's why. There was some pig-eyed private eye with his hand out and I had to give him a hundred and a quarter. If you don't get more than that, I have trouble sleeping tonight."

"It doesn't really sound right," Hazlitt said. "I'm not sure I follow what you're saying, but this is the kind of thing I either keep the information to myself or give it to you for nothing. I'm sorry I talked about money. I just found out tonight about going to have another baby, and it sort of threw me. The money part of it and everything else."

"My violin's out being fixed," Sam Murray said, a little cruelly. "Nobody's any better than anybody else. Here. This is yours."

He put two hundred dollars in Alf Hazlitt's coat pocket.

Now it was the next morning, and Sam was still in bed in his room at the hotel, having finished his breakfast and now finishing the story in the *Times*. In a left-handed sort of way, he had to admire the newspaper. Though it obviously intended to include world as well as local news, events beyond the immediate locale were relegated to the inside pages with a firm purpose. On page one, in addition to a separate story on the wedding of the daughter of Police Chief Martin Halverson, there was news of a gas war between local filling stations, the opening of the spring Ladies' Flower Exposition at the Rain Street Armory, the birth of a son at the Kamm Memorial Hospital to Mrs. W. W. Wright of Vista Road, and construction plans for an added wing at the South Road School. Hydrogen bombs, Congress, and disastrous tornado upheaval began on page two.

None of which reduced the size or the enthusiasm of the *Times's* audience. Among those reading the wiretap spread on page one was Mr. Andrew Fannell. He was not sure whether it made him unhappy or not.

CHAPTER NINE

L IKE SAM MURRAY, FANNELL HAD THE PAPER BROUGHT TO him with his breakfast as he reclined in bed; the paper was the same that Murray saw, but for Fannell the breakfast and the bed were both considerably better. Breakfast was brought on a rolling table by a manservant named Webbe. Fannell's bedroom was large, measuring thirty by twenty-five feet, but it was furnished in severe taste. The bed, overlarge and luxurious, stood in contrast to the simple walnut furnishings; the drapes at the window, though rich with weight, were subdued and seemed unobtrusive. And almost unreal was the realism of the square night table beside the bed, whose surface was unoccupied except for three black telephones.

There was a buzzing sound, and Fannell, dressed in a black silk robe over his pajamas, reached away from the breakfast tray and picked up the nearest phone. He said, "Yes?" and waited and then said, "Bring him on in." Then he went back to his breakfast, and in a short time there was a knock on the door. Fannell said, "Come," and the door opened and the manservant, Webbe, came in, escorting another man. The visitor was Harry Millburn.

"Hello, Andy," Millburn said. The round face and small eyes were one great worshipful hello. "How are you, Andy? You look fine this—"

"Now, damn it," Fannell said, "sit in the chair over there and talk to me when I ask you questions." He drew his napkin across his mouth. "What kind of a fellow is this Murray?"

"A cinch, you ask me," Millburn said. "A walking cinch. They got my name to him before he even left Port Gerard to come here, and he knows I'm the number one tap man and—"

"Stop it," Fannell said. "You're not number one. You're number six or seven."

Millburn moistened his lips. "You don't rate people like that. In my field—"

"In your field," Fannell said, "you're number six or seven. If you were any higher than that you would have beat this town a long time ago."

"This town treats me all right," Millburn said.

"I still know others I'd rather have than you," Fannell said. "That man Spindel in New York for one, but I can't get to him. So I settled for you. I compromised. Remember that."

Milburn lit a cigarette and looked around the room.

"Put the match in your pocket," Fannell said.

The private detective did as he was told, did it hastily. His face was a study.

"The ashes, too," Fannell said. "Murray got in touch with the paper, didn't he?"

"Yup," Millburn said. "Just the way you called it in advance."

"You took him to the place?"

"That's right."

Fannell wagged a finger. "You were holding out on me. You didn't tell me you knew what numbers were being tapped."

"I don't know where Murray found that out," Millburn said. "No?"

"Christ is my judge, Andy," Millburn said. "He found it out someplace, but not from me."

"You want me to believe that?"

"Andy," Millburn said, "I didn't *know* what numbers were being tapped."

Fannell looked at his nails. "That detective who told us about the raid—he said the numbers were taped up on the board."

Millburn nodded; he seemed agitated. "Somebody took those tapes down before I ever set foot in the place. Christ is my judge, Andy."

"Judy Chasen's phone," Fannell said musingly. "We ought to have a talk with her about that."

"*You* have a talk with her," Millburn said. "She's not talking to me."

Fannell nodded. "This man Murray. He's all eyes?"

"The most," Millburn said. "You ought to see him. He's right out of Dale Carnegie by Uncle Dan Beard. I was waiting for him to tell me you can make a fire by rubbing two pieces of wood together."

"You can," Fannell said, "if one of them's a match." He emptied his coffee cup.

"You just have to remember," Millburn said, "that no man works for a thing like an anti-crime commission without a reason."

"Maybe he's just a rugged individualist." Fannell made a husky noise in his throat. "An honest man."

"Maybe," Millburn said.

"Usually," Fannell said, "that type of fellow becomes a baseball umpire." He shot a look at Harry Millburn. "Now you laugh and say har, har, that's a good one, boss."

"I think we all have weaknesses," Harry Millburn said. "With this Murray I think we hit it right off."

"Money?"

"Women."

"He met Ellie?"

"He did."

"Liked her?"

"Very much."

"Well," Andy Fannell said. "Well, well, well. Murray isn't married, is he?"

"No," Millburn said. Hopelessly, and with as much elan as possible, he tapped the ashes of his cigarette into his suitcoat pocket. "Was once. Show girl."

"Every man the way he's gaited," Fannell said philosophically. "You know, people don't really understand the *choice* element."

Millburn said, "I beg your pardon?"

"You see?" Fannell said to him. "You don't understand it either."

"Choice, I don't understand," the private detective said.

"Every man," Andy Fannell said thoughtfully, "is limited. My theory is he's limited to two—two of the following: money, whisky, women, horses, honesty, hunting, and gin rummy. With you, it's money and gin rummy. With me, it's money and horses. With Murray it's honesty and women. They're all the same. I just don't think a man is constituted to make any kind of a career out of more than two of those things at any one time."

Millburn thought for a moment. "What about fishing and golf?"

"Secondary categories," Fannell said. "So he liked Ellie."

"Very much," Harry Millburn said. "I left them together for supper. He brought her home a little before midnight."

"What'd she tell him she does for a living?"

"Writes women's news for the paper."

Fannell moved his shoulders. "Now *that* was a damn fool thing to say. All he's got to do is call the paper—he's in touch with them half of every day anyway—and right away you're in trouble."

"No," Millburn said. He tapped his forehead significantly. "Give Harry credit where credit's due. I figure number one, it's so easy to check a thing like that that he won't think of checking it. Number two, if she's my sister and they say she doesn't work at the paper, he'll put two and two together and figure—very logically—that she works under an assumed name. Number three, if it comes to a jackpot, she can always tell him she was ashamed to say what she really does for a living."

"I'd be ashamed, too," Fannell said.

"Watch out," Millburn said. "She's my sister."

"Oh, for God's sake," Andy Fannell said.

"It was your idea, this business of putting Ellie onto Murray," Millburn said. "I hope you aren't forgetting that."

"Naturally," Fannell said. "I've already told you what we're trying to do with Mr. Murray."

"Neutralize him, whatever that means." Millburn was acutely aware of his cigarette's shortened length. "You want to let him make all the noise he can about wiretapping. You say it won't backfire. I don't know. What if he gets the state legislature interested?"

Fannell raised his eyebrows. "Let them. They'll investigate, and the police will tell them that wiretapping is essential to police work—which you and I know it isn't—and wiretapping will still be in business."

"Legal wiretapping?"

"Wiretapping," Fannell repeated.

"So what's the poop?" Millburn said. "What's the reason for encouraging him at all?"

"Read the morning paper," Fannell said. "The answer's there."

"I read the morning paper. It's full of wiretapping."

"Head of the class for you," the gambler said. "Full of wiretapping. Takes people's minds off other things."

"Like just for instance?"

"Like just for instance who killed the old judge."

CHAPTER TEN

"Like just for instance," Sam Murray said to himself, looking in the mirror as he shaved, "who killed the old judge?"

The face in the mirror replied, "None of your business, bright boy. You have other problems. Including love."

"Love, love," Sam said into the mirror.

"Hooray for love," the mirror said. "No one's ever too blasé for love."

"Ach," Sam said to the mirror. "You dog, you. Maybe you score with that broad tonight."

The phone rang for the third time this crowded morning. First it had been a man who said he was Joseph Thomas, the county prosecutor, who wanted to co-operate 100% with the state anti-crime commission. Then it was Ben Phillips, who said he was running for alderman and wanted to co-operate 100% with the state anti-crime commission.

"This will be another liar," Murray told himself, and went and picked up the phone.

It was a woman—not, he realized at once, the woman he wanted to hear from. He thought of last night with Ellie Millburn. She had told him she would call, but from the paper, not from home; for reasons that seemed obvious, she did not wish him to call her.

The voice Murray heard now was not unpleasant—but it was not Ellie's voice. "Mr. Murray?"

"That's right," he said.

"Thank God I got you," the voice said. "It said on the television you were staying at the Kamm."

Sam Murray scratched his ear and said into the telephone, "Well. Who's this?"

"Judith Chasen."

"The one in the paper?"

"That's what I wanted to talk to you about."

"All right," Sam said, "if there's something you can tell me. There's nothing I can tell you. I don't know any more than you do."

There was silence at the other end, and Sam said, "What's more, I don't want to know."

Again there was silence, but after a time, her voice sounding far away now, Judith Chasen said, "All right. I'm sorry."

"Don't be sorry," Murray said.

"I thought you could help me."

"I can't. I'm running out of money. If I pay for any more home hints in this town I'll have to wire dad for more."

"What are you talking about?" the girl said. "I asked for help, not money."

"I don't know what help I can give you."

"Nobody else can either."

"I wouldn't say that."

"Nobody else will. Put it that way, if you want to. The police ask me a lot of stupid questions and the photographers want to take pictures of me in my nightgown."

"My, my," Murray said to her. "And we've barely been introduced. Pardon the pun."

The silence again; it seemed to Sam Murray he ought to say something, and he cleared his throat and said, "Look, it isn't the business of the anti-crime commission to look into things on a personal basis. We're interested in telling the public that your phone was tapped, but it could be anybody's phone. It's the tap part, not the who or the why."

The voice named Judith Chasen said, "Then why did you tell the paper about me?"

"I didn't," Murray said. "I gave the paper the numbers that had been tapped, but I didn't know whose they were."

"I'll bet Fannell knew," the girl said. She said it in a way that was not wholly directed at Sam Murray on the other end of the phone, but when she said it he became newly interested, and angry with himself for not having thought of this sooner.

He said, "You work for him, don't you?"

"I sing at the Holiday Inn."

"That means you work for Fannell."

"You don't know him very well, do you?"

"Don't know him at all. Know of him."

"It's not a nice thing to tell somebody they 'work' for Fannell," Judith Chasen said, and the way she said it put the word "work" in quotes. "All I do is sing at his place."

"Does he sign your salary check?"

"Yes."

"Well," Murray said, and was going to continue with some smart crack, addressed not only to the girl on the phone but to girl singers and show girls in general, who had been his natural enemies ever since his divorce. Instead, though, he said, "Can you introduce me to Fannell?"

"Yes."

"When?"

"Tonight, if you want."

"At the place? The Holiday Inn?"

"All right," the girl said. There was a pause, and then she said, "You don't want to help me with this other business?"

"I don't know what I can do," Murray said. "All right. The hell with it. Where are you now?"

"Home," Judith Chasen said. She gave him the address.

"How long will you be there?"

"A while."

"I'll come on out," Murray said. "You can tell me about it."

Something in his voice caused her to bristle. "You're sure I'm not troubling you."

"I'm not sure," Sam Murray said, "but there's nothing else to do around here except talk to D.A.s on the phone."

After he had hung up the phone, Murray brooded for a bit, then put in a long-distance call to Walter Lord in Port Gerard. Lord was a former FBI agent, brought in with Murray four years ago to form the nucleus of the office staff for the anti-crime commission. The board of directors of the commission itself was composed of bankers, newspaper executives, doctors, realtors, industrialists, and so forth—men and women who were publicly dedicated to to the eradication of crime, but who had never, specifically, been brought to the test. It was all right so long as you were exposing juvenile delinquency and the Mafia. It was a question, though, whether an exposé by the commission's working staff of wrongdoing in a certain steel company would sit well with that member of the commission's board of directors who was the steel company's vice-president.

Certainly, if the commission's own board of directors could not be counted on to back up the staff work, then there would be no place to turn. The very formation of the anti-crime commission had incurred the well-masked dislike of every police chief and district attorney in the state. The very existence of a privately-supported anti-crime commission was in itself a reflection on the existing official machineries for law and order.

But Walter Lord, a working staff member, was very happy to hear from Sam Murray.

"Met Joe Thomas?"

"The county prosecutor?" Murray rubbed at his ear lobe. "Not yet. He called up. Told me how happy he was to have a visit from the anti-crime commission."

"Wear your bulletproof vest," Lord said. "The wire services picked up a little bit of the tap story from there. Played up some dame who sings at Fannell's place."

"I'm leaving to have a talk with her now," Murray said.

"What about that guy Millburn?"

"Seems very anxious to help," Murray said. "Met him last night. He appears to have a lot of talent for his particular line of work."

"What else has he got?"

"A sister. She works for the paper."

"Well," Walter Lord said from the other end of the phone. "I'd say offhand that Sam Murray was about par for the course. Two days. Two dames."

"Knock it off," Murray said. "The one who sings is going to introduce me to Fannell."

"Fannell and I are old buddies," Walter Lord said. "I did some work on him when they were trying to deport him. If you're going out to the Holiday Inn, you better get a corner table."

Murray nodded into the phone. He said, "Maybe I'll get married."

"The singer?"

"Millburn's sister."

"You just met her."

"Maybe that's the way to do it," Murray said. "You can't prove it by me."

"You can't prove anything by you," Lord said. "That's what made you such a good cop. However, I wish to remind you of the stated purpose of the anti-crime commission."

"Yes," Murray said. "Wiretapping."

"No, I meant the other purpose," Lord said. "We've launched a new campaign against venereal disease. Take care of yourself."

They said good-by and hung up, and Murray turned and went to the closet to pick out a tie. He was waiting for the phone to ring, but it did not, and after a time he took the piece of paper on which he had written Judith Chasen's address and went out.

Going down in the elevator, and in the taxicab on the way out to the girl's place, he remembered that the phone call he had been anticipating was one from Ellie Millburn. His mind retraced events of the night previous. The only thing he could say positively about Ellie was that he preferred her to her brother Harry. He also was interested, almost in a clinical way, in finding out more about her, and he wondered how their date tonight would turn out.

The movie they had seen, he recalled, had been one of those documentary westerns with its lone-wolf hero riding silently into the troubled town. Sam Murray was not easily swayed by the world of make-believe, but it was not too hard for him to transfer the role of the hero in the picture to his present part in real life. True, he had not ridden a horse into this town—had arrived, instead, on the local from Port Gerard—but he had come to help the troubled, and he would leave the same way, alone.

"Ah," he said now, and remembered what he had forgotten the night before. Leaving Ellie's apartment he had meant to look to see whether a plain-clothes man was staked out in a car across the street.

Now, for some reason, probably belated compensation, he did look carefully to see if there was a stake-out in front of the rooming house where Judith Chasen lived. But it was a quiet street, well removed from the center of the city, and the occasional parked cars, the sheen of their surfaces mottled by the shadow of great forgiving elm trees that lined the pavement, all were empty.

The rooming house had three floors; downstairs there were mail boxes with buzzer buttons, and Sam pushed the button over the box marked CHASEN-DEER, and soon an answering buzz unlocked the inner door; and, going in, he saw the girl looking down at him from the landing of the second floor.

"Hi," Sam said, "Miss Chasen?"

"Mr. Murray?" she said. "Come on up."

She was wearing a bandanna and a green sweater and gray slacks, and she had slippers on her feet, so that when he reached the second floor it seemed he was looking down at her from a great height. Actually, he surmised, she was at least five-foot-three. Her face, which except for a little lipstick was devoid of makeup, looked clean and young; the sweater was of the floppy type that did not clue him as to her figure, and her hair was swathed in the bandanna.

Sam said, "Are you blond or brunette?"

"Blond," she said. "Naturally."

"You mean naturally naturally or naturally of course?"

"Take your best hold," the girl said, and held open the door. "Don't you wear a hat? I thought all detectives wore hats."

"I'm not a detective," Sam said.

"Oh? It said in the paper—"

"It said in the paper—what seems to be, I might add, the most widely-read paper in the world—that I worked for the anti-crime commission."

"Isn't that being a detective?"

"Only sometimes and never officially. I used to be a detective."

"Did you wear a hat then?"

"Cut it out," Sam Murray said to her. He looked around the living room of the suite. To the left there was a dining area and the entrance to a small kitchen; to the right, the bedroom section. He said, "Where's Deer?"

"Who?"

"The one on the mail box."

"Oh," Judith Chasen said. "You mean Marcia."

"Marcia?"

"My roommate."

Murray nodded. "Well?"

"Out. She works."

"Where?"

"Is that your business?"

"Yes."

"Pretty positive, aren't you?"

"Play games, all right," Murray said. "Scrabble?"

Judith Chasen sat down on the couch facing him and said, "She works for the newspaper."

Sam Murray reached across his face and rubbed at his ear. "This is the damnedest town I ever saw. Population forty-five thousand and every other woman in town works for that one-lung paper."

"What's that?" the girl said. "Everybody works for the paper?"

"Never mind," Sam said. "What does she do? Women's news? Home hints? Graduate of the Missouri School of Journalism?"

Judith Chasen looked at him, puzzled. "She's the adtaker. You know. When you have a house for rent or a death notice or a car or a washing machine. That's Marcia's department."

"Oh," Sam Murray said. He looked relieved. "Do you have anything to drink?"

"In the morning?"

"I won't drink alone."

"Then you won't drink."

Murray grinned. "Okay. Just testing. One-two-three, woof-woof, hello, Max."

The girl watched him speculatively. "Don't you want to know where the telephone is?"

"No. Why should I?"

"I thought—"

"There's nothing to see but a telephone. Assuming you have your own."

"Of course I have."

"It's a rooming house," Murray pointed out. "Some of them have public phones in the hall." He rubbed his ear. "But that wouldn't be you, would it? The phone's listed under your name."

"We're not making much progress," the girl said. "Are we?"

"Not much outside of I know you don't drink in the morning." Sam stood up. There was a spinet against the far wall with some sheet music on the stand. He went over and started thumbing through a batch of lead sheets. "Guitar chords," he observed. "Good." He looked up. "I can play piano from the guitar chords. Not from the notes, though."

"Well," the girl said. "Are we going to have a concert?"

"Maybe. You married?"

"No."

"Been married before?"

"No."

"How old?"

The girl stood up and walked to the window. She looked back at Sam Murray. "You really have to know, don't you?"

"You asked me to help you."

She squared her shoulders. "I'm twenty-seven. You can smoke if you want to."

"No, thanks," Sam said. "Steady boy friend?"

"Not quite."

"What does that mean?"

"Not quite."

"What's his name?"

"Ben Phillips. You wouldn't know him."

"There's a Ben Phillips running for alderman."

"That's the one."

"Does he call you up much?"

"Some."

"Sexy conversations?"

Judith Chasen started to say something, but a thought struck her, and her face had an introspective smile. "You don't know Ben."

"I don't know you, either. You have any money?"

"Not much. Just enough from week to week."

"Anybody trying to shake you down? Blackmail you?"

"No."

"Is there anybody who might learn something from tapping your line?"

"I don't know."

"What about Fannell?"

"He leaves me alone."

"How old is Deer?"

"Who?"

"Marcia. The roommate."

"Thirty. Thirty-two. I'm not sure."

"Married?"

"Separated."

"Going to get a divorce?"

"I think so. Why don't you ask her?"

"I'm not that interested. What did you mean, you didn't know?"

She looked at him.

"A minute ago," Murray said, "I asked you if anybody—some guy or one of your prospective keepers or somebody—would have any reason for tapping your phone and you said, 'I don't know.'"

"I didn't mean anything by it." Her eyes were hot. "I said 'I don't know' meaning I don't know of any reason. No reason in the world. And I don't like that word."

"What word is that?"

"Keeper. Maybe I work for a living. Did that ever occur to you?"

"Yes," Murray said reasonably. "It occurred to me. I married one of your kind one time. It didn't last."

"Oh," Judith Chasen said. "One of my kind. You know all about my kind, don't you?"

"You sing in a saloon. Right?"

"What if I do?"

"Then don't tell me I don't know your kind," Sam Murray said to her.

She came across the room toward him. "I'll tell you something about my kind. If somebody insults me in that stinking place where I work, they throw him out."

"Only if it's a drunk," Sam said mildly.

"Because they don't talk that way sober."

"I do."

She walked over to where he was sitting and slapped his face. She was close to tears. "Get out of here," she said.

Sam stood up. "I came here because you asked me."

"I didn't ask for this."

"You asked for help."

"You were the only one I could think of. I wanted to know about the phone. That's all I wanted to know. I didn't ask you to tell me about my kind."

"Your kind," Sam Murray said, "usually gets its phones tapped."

"Thanks. You've told me a lot."

Murray paused at the door. "Only in this case," he said, "I'd say it's ten to one you'll find Marcia Deer is after her husband for alimony and he's had a private detective put a tap on her phone—which happens to be the phone listed under your name—to get something on her. They might be tapping your phone to get something on this guy Phillips, but ordinarily you'd first want to find out whether they're tapping *his* phone. See?"

She stared at him.

"And tonight," Sam Murray said, "I would like to come to the Holiday Inn so you can introduce me to Mr. Fannell."

"I can't stop you," Judith Chasen said. Her voice was low. "It's a free country."

"That it is," Sam said. "A man can get his face slapped almost anywhere."

He did not say good-by, merely nodded his head, for he thought it would be difficult to improve on his last remark as an exit line. At the bottom of the stairs, he turned and looked back and half saluted in the direction of Judith Chasen, with what he hoped was the proper kind of smile on his face.

Then he went outside, walked two blocks before he found a cab, and rode back to the Kamm Hotel.

Riding in the cab, he believed he had been right in saying that it was Judith Chasen's roommate that the tap was on; he wondered, too, about the other taps—three lines at the metals company, two at the stock broker's—and whether they lent themselves to so logical a solution. Industrial espionage? It was a factor. It happened. Competitive information by tapping the metals people, advance information by tapping the brokerage. He nodded to himself, pleased.

And was none the less pleased when he got back to the hotel, for in his box at the room clerk's desk was a telephone slip saying that Miss Millburn had called, saying also that she would call back—that he should not call her.

"Ellie's scared," Sam said to himself aloud as he waited for the elevator. "She's scared and Our Hero here has to do something to make her less scared. That's why Our Hero's here. The hell with the wiretapping."

At least, he thought, going up in the elevator, Ellie had her points. One did not meet a girl like this every day. No, one was more likely to meet a girl where the reaction was bad and instant and automatic—as with this show girl Judy Chasen. You were honest with a girl like Judy. You said what came to your mind. You helped her out. And she belted you for it. It happened.

Well, he told himself, he would use Judy Chasen as a means of getting to meet the fabled Mr. Andy Fannell. And then he would not mess with Judy Chasen any more, and relatively speaking he was just as well off for having been in this town twenty-four hours, stirring things up, and getting away with no more than a slap across the face.

He opened the door to his room, and in a movement of fine reflex conditioning, traced to his years as a detective, twisted with his shoulder away from the man waiting there on the left.

But there were two of them, and the other man hit him across the temple with something dull and hard, and he went unconscious, knowing only dimly, in the moment before he stopped all thinking, that at least when she slapped you Judy Chasen was a lady.

CHAPTER ELEVEN

I N THE DETECTIVE STORIES, THE HERO ALWAYS CAME AWAKE
to find himself alone in the room except for a naked woman
who was also dead, and a smoking hot pistol in his hand. Sam
Murray came awake to find himself alone in the room except for
nothing, and what woke him was the telephone. Or at least, it was
ringing when he came to.

The side of his head felt warm rather than painful. He got to
the side of the bed and sat there while the phone rang two more
times. Then he picked it up and said hello.

"Sam? It's Ellie."

"Oh," he said.

"Hello, baby," she said.

"What time is it?" Sam said.

"Four o'clock," Ellie said. "No. Not quite. How have you
been, baby?"

"I was all right up to lunch."

"Oh," Ellie said. "Poor baby. Something disagree with you?"

"Yes," Sam said, and did not say more. Talking was something of an effort for him. Sitting there with the phone held to
his ear, Sam appreciated the physiological difference between the
mind and the head. His mind was clear. His head felt like something in the shot put. He said, "I'm supposed to meet a fellow at
the Holiday Inn tonight."

"Oh." Her voice went flat. "Without me?"

"Hell, no," Sam said. "With you. Where do I pick you up? When?"

There was a pause. Then the girl said, "It'd be better if you didn't call for me." Her voice brightened. "I can meet you there. Harry can bring me."

"Yes," Sam said. "All right. How's Harry?"

"Just fine," Ellie said.

"Good old Harry," Sam said.

"What time?" Ellie said.

"I don't know," Sam said. "Late-ish, so I can get my meeting out of the way. Ten o'clock too late?"

"Depends on your plans for the rest of the evening." She was throwing the ball to him.

He caught it one-handed, like Long George Kelly. "What I've got in mind, ten o'clock's just right. I mean for openers."

"I was hoping you'd say that," Ellie said. Her voice was newly soft. "See you then, baby."

"'By, lover," Sam said, and kissed the mouthpiece and hung up the phone. He sat there for a time, then picked up the phone again and asked for room service. When he got them, he asked for a bucket of ice.

"Yes, sir," room service said. "A bucket of ice. Set-ups for two?"

"No," Sam said.

"One?"

"No."

"Just ice?"

"That's right."

"I see," the voice said. "You want a refill. You've already had room service."

"I had room service just before lunch," Sam said, "and I must say you do the patrons up brown. As of now, all I want is ice."

"Ice," the voice repeated.

Sam took the last chance. "And a bottle of bourbon—make it Harper—and one set-up."

"Right away, sir," the voice said.

Sam hung up, and felt his head and went to the radio that was on the bureau across the room and dropped a quarter in. The radio hummed to life, and he heard a man singing,

> "You've never known a sky so blue,
> You've never felt a breeze so fair,
> Till you've seen springtime in Aimerly.
> What a happy time there!"

"My God," Sam said aloud. "The damn town's even got a local song." He listened to the rest of it.

> "You've never heard a robin sing,
> You've never touched a lover's hand,
> Till you've seen springtime in Aimerly,
> That springtime land."

"Now the bridge," Sam said.

> "Every gentle flower
> Bends to kiss the sun;
> Never mind the hour,
> Springtime is never done."

Sam said, "Oh, for God's sake."

> "You've never known a finer home,
> A more delightful place to be,

Than when it's springtime
In Aimerly."

There was a musical interlude now, and then, as the voice went into the words again, there was a rap at the door and Sam went to admit the man from room service. The man from room service was a gray, humorless little man. Sam looked at him and said, "Native here?"

"Fifty-six years," the little man said.

"Hark to the wireless," Sam said. "They're playing your song."

The man listened. His face brightened and he set down the tray he carried. "That's one of our lads doing the singing," he said. "Hoolihan, the singing policeman."

"It figured," Sam said, and let the man have a dollar tip.

He put a piece of ice to his head and drank the whisky neat. Outside, it was cold and glowering, and there was a suggestion of snow. "Springtime in Aimerly," Sam Murray muttered to himself, and then the phone rang again. This time it was Joe Thomas, the county prosecutor.

"Sam," he said. "Is it all right if I call you Sam?"

"Fine," Murray said.

"You can call me Joe," Thomas said.

"Thanks, Joe," Sam said.

"I'd like to talk to you, Sam."

"Any time, Joe."

"So would the grand jury."

"Whose?"

"Mine."

"Oh?"

"Yes," Thomas said. "We're interested in finding out all you know about this—ah—raid."

"All I know was in this morning's paper."

"Then you won't mind telling the jury?"

"Not at all."

"I'd like to know, too," Thomas said—he was using the pronouns "I," "we," and "they" interchangeably to denote that he and the grand jury were indeed one—"why you didn't come to me, or to the police, instead of going to the papers."

"Go to the police?" Murray said. "They're the ones who made the raid."

"I didn't know anything about it," Thomas said stiffly. "I'm supposed to be the county prosecutor."

"Have you talked to your chief of police?"

"He was attending his daughter's wedding."

"That's right," Murray said. "Celia. I read about it in the paper." A nagging feeling came to the back of his mind. There was something about that newspaper—something he wanted to link up with something else—and he could not discover what it was. It did not have to do with the wiretap story. It was something else.

"Do you always operate this way?" Thomas said. "I mean, in public? I'm just asking, Sam."

"That's the function of the anti-crime commission," Murray said. "Joe, you sound a little different this afternoon. This morning when you called, you wanted to cooperate a hundred per cent."

"I still do, Sam," Thomas said. "I still do. The purpose of this call now is just to find out whether *you* want to co-operate with *me*."

"I'll tell you everything I know," Murray said again.

"And the jury, too?"

"Sure."

"We'd like to know the source of your information as well. If you want to save time, you can tell me over the phone now, if you'd like."

"I wouldn't like," Sam said.

"No?" Thomas said.

"No," Murray said. "What possible good would it do you to know?"

"I'm not talking about *my* good, Sam," Thomas said. "But the jury might ask you. You know how it is."

"I know the jury asks what the D.A. tells them to ask."

"Well, now," Thomas said cheerily, "I wouldn't say that. There's a law in this state saying no newspaperman has to reveal the source of his information."

"It's a good law," Sam said. "More states ought to have it."

"Uh-huh," Thomas said. "But that law doesn't apply to people from the anti-crime commission."

"It's springtime in Aimerly," Murray said into the phone. "And the D.A.'s going fishing."

"Now, Sam," Thomas said. "Let's not get huffy with each other. It isn't going to come down to anything like that. We'll get along just fine, you and I. After all, we're both on the same side in this fight."

"Good to know it," Murray said. "While we're swearing undying loyalty, you might tell the jury some citizen of this fair town flogged me one time on the side of the head with a blunt instrument, noonish today."

"What?" Thomas said. "Are you kidding?"

"No."

"Where'd it happen?"

"Right here in the room. I opened the door and bang."

"Who was it?"

"How the hell do I know?"

"I wish you could give me a description, Sam," the prosecutor said.

"I went bye-bye," Murray said. "The guy knocked me out. As a matter of fact there were two of them. They worked the combination."

"Two men, you say," Thomas said.

"That's right."

"You know something?" Thomas said. "I wish you'd told me this right away, as soon as you picked up the phone right now."

"Why?"

"Well, I would have come right out and suggested what I'll suggest now anyway. Look, Sam, I'll tell the jury you don't know anything outside of what was in the paper, and what the hell. Your work's done here. Why don't you hop a train before somebody gets real mean? There are boys around this town who play for keeps, and somebody's not happy having you here."

"That I do believe," Murray said.

"Tell you what," Thomas said. "I'll send a car to get you from the hotel to the station and you'll have police protection all the way. There's a train for Port Gerard around five-thirty. Get you out of harm's reach before you even know it."

"Sweet of you to think of me," Murray said. "But I bid no trump. I have to stay over at least tonight."

"For God's sake, why?"

"I got a date with a dame."

"Oh, baby, what a nut," Thomas said. "Next thing you'll tell me you're meeting her at Fannell's place out on the highway."

"The Holiday Inn?" Murray said.

"That's the name of it," Thomas said.

"That's where I'll be," Murray said.

"Sam," Thomas said, "do me a favor. Leave town, will you please? As a favor to me?"

CHARLES EINSTEIN

"Gee, Joe," Murray said. "You don't know this girl or you wouldn't talk like that."

"I know Fannell," Thomas said darkly. "Are you really serious? I mean it. I'll let you off from the jury. You stay here that jury's going to make you sweat. I mean it. If somebody doesn't put a knife in you first."

The sound from the radio in Murray's room was reminiscent. He said into the phone, "Wait a minute, Joe," and went and turned the volume up, then went back to the telephone.

> "You've never known a sky so blue,
> You've never felt a breeze so fair,
> Till you've seen springtime in Aimerly.
> What a happy time there!"

"Hear that, Joe?" Murray said into the phone. "That's Hoolihan, the singing policeman."

CHAPTER TWELVE

THE HOLIDAY INN WAS A PLACE TO SEE. THERE WAS MONEY, much money, in Aimerly County, else Andy Fannell would not be operating here. He himself had directed the redecorating of the Holiday Inn when he took it over, in his nephew's name, of course, just before the outbreak of World War II. Downstairs was the night-club floor and Fannell's suite of private offices; upstairs the card and roulette rooms and several tasteful bedrooms where Fannell, who did not traffic in organized prostitution, might nonetheless arrange for the entertainment of good friends.

And who was not Andy Fannell's good friend? It was tough to say, though things were a little more certain and easily handled while Steve Yaros, Joe Thomas's chief investigator and visiting bag man, was alive. This was the stake that Fannell had in the forthcoming local election. He wished to see Ben Phillips, the rebel candidate, defeated, so that Thomas would have a free hand to appoint the right kind of successor to Yaros as his chief investigator and go-between.

Meanwhile, though, Fannell had to wait and see. There were times when he wished he had access to the files and information possessed by old Judge Yorty. Without sufficient information, he could not play the kind of role he wanted in the local campaign—not that he could not get to politicians, which he had already done, but he would have preferred a sure thing. And that was why he was at least pleased that, given a choice of local headlines, the paper now was concerned with wiretapping rather than the death of Judge Yorty. This man Murray, from the state anti-crime commission, was going to do everything in his power to see to it that the local tap situation became a matter for statewide concern. That was Murray's mission; and Fannell would do everything in his power to see that Murray succeeded, because the more general the tap probe became then the less local it would seem, and with Phillips spotlighting local issues in his campaign it was worth the momentary local spotlight on wiretapping to achieve the two more important ends of enlarging the tap thing beyond local proportions and minimizing the death of the judge.

Who was not Andy Fannell's good friend? Well, under present circumstances there were several people he would rather see in the Holiday Inn than Ben Phillips. But Phillips was courting Judy Chasen, the singer, and reported for duty religiously each evening at eight-thirty. Phillips was a thin, intense man, perhaps thirty-eight or forty years of age, who ran that string of liquor stores in town. He had started with one store when he came to Aimerly from New York during the war, but Aimerly liked its whisky and the times had been good to him.

As the evenings wore on and the clubroom of the Holiday Inn became more and more crowded, Ben Phillips would sit there at his table, over by the wall quite close to the stage, drumming his fingers idly in time to the dance music and the music for the acts—all except Judy's, when he would sit instead in mute concentration, staring at her through the bright-dull smoke haze in the room. Occasionally, she came to his table to sit with him for a time between sets, but generally he sat there alone until her final set at two o'clock, and then would drive her home.

He was a lonely man, Ben Phillips was. Outside of a married sister, he had no family to call his own, and love, up to this relatively late stage in his life, had passed him by. Even now he was not sure he was in love with Judy Chasen, nor any more sure that she loved him.

But it was something, and something was better than nothing. Sometimes he said to himself that the only reason he had entered politics was to have something to fill the hours in his life.

At that, alderman was a lowly starting point, even in so fortuitously vital an election as the one now being campaigned in Aimerly. But a man could go up from alderman. The important thing was to win the first one.

And now, sitting at his table in the Holiday Inn, Ben Phillips looked around the half-empty room and flashed a leathery smile to those scattered customers who, he could only assume, might be his constituents-to-be.

The first show—the dinner show—went on a little after nine o'clock. Ben waited impatiently, waiting for Judy Chasen to make her appearance. He wanted to hear her sing *Springtime in Aimerly;* he loved this town, Ben did, and thought it wonderful that a city should have its own private song.

His attention was drawn away from the stage, though, by the hovering presence of a waiter. The waiter said, "There's a man here who wants to meet you."

Galvanized by candidacy, Ben came smiling to his feet. The man behind the waiter was tall and sad-looking; his suit was not as highly pressed as it might have been, and to Ben's sharp first scrutiny it seemed the stranger might even be a little drunk.

"Sam Murray," the newcomer said, and they shook hands. "I talked to you on the phone earlier today."

"Well," Phillips said. "Well, well, well. Sit down, Mr. Murray. Have you eaten?"

"No," Murray said. "How's the food here?"

"If I wasn't running for alderman I'd tell you," Ben Phillips said. He let Murray sit down first. "Well. A real honest-to-God crime-buster. You don't know what a pleasure this is."

"Thank you," Murray said.

"Especially in this town," Phillips said. "A man who's running against crime around here can feel awful lonesome sometimes."

"Especially here," Murray said. He was studying the menu.

"Hell, man," Ben Phillips said. "I only come here for Judy's sake. Judy Chasen. The singer."

"We've met," Murray said.

"You know Judy?"

Murray looked at him briefly. "She consulted me today. About her phone."

"Now, there's something," Phillips said. "What do you think about that?"

"Not a hell of a lot," Murray said.

"I mean," Phillips said, "the fact that things like that could go on. Now, why would anybody want to tap Judy's phone?"

"Beats me," Murray said. "Maybe it was a divorce business with her roommate."

"That's right," Ben Phillips said. "The roommate. Marian."

"Marcia," Murray said. "Marcia Deer."

Phillips looked at him in open admiration. "Man, is that something," he said. "Here I've known Judy all this time, and I can never remember the roommate's name. You meet her one day and bang."

"I beg your pardon," Murray said dimly.

"Your memory, man," Phillips said to him. "How do you do it?"

"I think I'll have the chopped steak," Murray said. "My memory? Nothing to it. Get yourself hit on the head one time before lunch every day. That's all."

"Man," Ben Phillips said, "you're a card."

"Baby-boy," Murray said. "Can we get the waiter? Did you eat?"

"I'll get him," Phillips said, and half rose in his chair to signal the waiter. The waiter came over and Phillips said, "A chopped steak for my good friend here. How do you want it, man?"

Murray rubbed cross-handed at his ear. He said, "Medium-rare, with a salad." He turned to Phillips. "What about you?"

"Just a nice tossed green salad," Phillips said. The waiter went away and Phillips said, "You know, if they make me alderman, I'm going to look into this whole business of wiretapping."

"Good," Murray said.

"If you ask me," Phillips said, "it's a violation of the Fourth Amendment to the Constitution."

"Probably is," Sam Murray said. "I'm not in favor of it."

"The trouble is," Phillips said, "wiretapping does do some good."

Murray looked at him. "It does? When? Where?"

"Well, man," Phillips said. "Suppose I murdered somebody. If you were a cop, wouldn't you want to tap my phone for the evidence?"

"If you murdered somebody," Murray said, "I gather you wouldn't be talking about it on the phone."

Phillips thought for a moment. Then he said, "Well, the police have got to have *some* excuse."

"They do," Murray said. "To get a legal tap, you have to go in front of a judge and say, 'I, such-and-such a law-enforcement officer, hereby request permission to tap the phone of so-and-so because I have reasonable grounds to believe that evidence of the following crime may thus be obtained.' Or words exactly to that effect. Then the judge signs the order—if it's the right judge, he won't even read it, because if there's any kickback he doesn't want to know whose phone was going to be tapped. Matter of fact, at the other extreme, a judge can refuse to sign the order. Lots of them do. One of them in New York threw an assistant D.A. out of his court and made a public statement saying the cops were doing too much of this kind of thing." Murray wished he had thought to order himself a before-dinner drink. He had this ruefully in mind as he pursued his subject with Phillips. "So what do cops do with wiretaps? They pile up paperwork, mainly, to make it look like they're busy on a case. Or they'll tap a rival politician—" Phillips winced, but Murray went on—" or maybe a bookmaker. Why do you tap a bookmaker? You already know the guy's making book. So what do you want with a tap? You want to know how much business the book's doing so you can know whether or not the book's paying the right amount of protection money."

Ben Phillips was wide-eyed. He said, "You know what this is? You know what all this is? It's ammunition, that's what it is. Ammunition for me!"

"Good luck," Sam Murray told him.

"Good luck," a voice from near by said, and both Murray and Ben Phillips looked over at the adjoining table. A small, bespectacled man sat there, smiling at them uncertainly. His body seemed to weave, as if on the receiving end of a series of spirit messages.

"Good luck," he said again, louder this time. Then he recognized Phillips. "Why, hello, there, Ben."

"Hello, Vernon," Phillips said. He looked a trifle embarrassed.

"Who's your friend?" the little man named Vernon said. He squinted carefully at Sam Murray.

"This is Mr. Murray, Vernon," Ben Phillips said.

"There was a Mr. Murray in the paper," Vernon said.

"This is the same one," Phillips said.

"From the anti-crime commission," Vernon said.

"That's right," Phillips said.

Vernon got up from his chair and leaned over to Sam Murray, "Boy," he said, "am I glad to see you!"

"Why don't you ask your friend to join us?" Murray said to Phillips.

"I'm embarrassed," Phillips said.

"Come over and sit with us," Murray said. "Is Vernon your first or last name?"

"Both," Vernon Vernon said, and came over and sat down, bringing his drink with him. "Mr. Murray, I want you to know you couldn't be in better company. This is the Honest Government candidate right here. Ben Phillips."

"Vernon is an eye doctor," Ben Phillips said to Murray. "He broke up with his wife."

"On the town ever since," Vernon said. He turned to Murray. "Aren't you drinking?"

"No," Murray said bitterly.

"Now, I had a patient today," Vernon Vernon, the eye doctor, said. "Came in and wanted her eyes tested—I tell you a real knockout of a broad—and she's got the same problem I've got—split up with her mate—and the next thing you know we've made a little date-eroo. Make time while you're young, I always say." He slugged bemusedly at his drink. "Of course, I'm forty-two. If it hadn't been for Ben here opening up one of his liquor stores right next door to my office, I'd have never got to meet you, Mr. Murray."

"It's a small world," Sam Murray said. His head still hurt him.

"But being from the anti-crime commission," Vernon said to him, "I want your actual opinion. Do you think what I'm doing's a crime?"

"What are you doing?"

Vernon waved an expansive hand. "Making a date with a patient."

"Oh, for God's sake," Murray said.

"Well," the eye doctor said patiently, "it seems to me that's what you anti-crime fellows are in business for. I can't ask the police for *their* opinion, or the Good Citizens' League, or even my lawyer. *He* ain't no help a-tall. But I figure I need advice. Where's the logical place to go? The anti-crime commission, says I."

"You mustn't mind Vernon," Ben Phillips said to Murray. "He's a little the worse for drink."

"I envy him," Murray said.

"Besides," Phillips said, "he has a peculiar idea of what it is anti-crime commissions do."

"He's no different than most people," Murray said. The waiter came with the food, and at that moment the orchestra struck a fanfare, the juggler who had occupied the stage disappeared, and, with the lights turning blue and soft, Judy Chasen came out.

It was really a production. Staring at her, close though the table was to the stage, Sam found it difficult to believe that this was the same girl who had met him in a floppy sweater and slapped his face for him earlier this same day. She was beautiful now. Her hair was swept back, and she wore a black velvet evening dress off the shoulders and cut whitely low. There was applause from the floor, now more than half filled with patrons, and the orchestra struck its lead-in, and Judy started to sing, at half the tempo Sam expected,

> "You've never known a sky so blue,
> You've never felt a breeze so fair,
> Till you've seen springtime in Aimerly.
> What a happy time there!"

She came to the bridge:

> "Every gentle flower
> Bends to kiss the sun—"

There was an audible sob from Vernon Vernon, the eye doctor. "I love that song," he said. "I love it." His body quaked.

"Bends to kiss the sun," Sam Murray said. "Now is that a hell of a line? I ask you?"

"Ssshh!" Ben Phillips said in annoyance. "Judy's singing."

"I need another drink," Vernon Vernon said.

"Ssssh!" Phillips said.

Sam Murray signaled for the waiter and pointed to Vernon's glass. Judy was still singing. Vernon said, "It makes me want to cry."

"Will you be quiet?" Phillips said.

"Gloria," Vernon said. "Gloria."

"Who?" Sam Murray said.

"Gloria," Vernon said. "The name of my patient."

"Ah, please," Ben Phillips said.

Vernon put a mysterious finger to his lips and gave Sam Murray the look of an utter conspirator.

Murray nodded solemnly.

Judy sang,

> "You've never known a finer home,
> A more delightful place to be,
> Than when it's springtime
> In Aimerly."

Then she went through it again, humming this time. Sam Murray went to work on his food and watched Ben Phillips's face as Judy worked. *The guy's got a case on her,* he told himself. He doubted that Judy was entirely reciprocal. The way she had talked about Phillips today, a couple of the things she had said, suggested this to Murray.

"She does it better," Murray said aloud, "than Hoolihan, the singing policeman."

Vernon Vernon came to life. He was, Murray realized now with force, quite drunk. He began to sing, to the tune *of* Columbia, the Gem of the Ocean:

"Oh, Hoolihan the sing-ing policeman
The symbol of the brave and the free!"

"The shrine of each patriot's devotion," Sam said to him.

"In the lovely town of Aim-erly," Vernon sang back.

Sam and Ben Phillips had finished their supper by the time Judy Chasen wound up her set. She walked directly over to their table.

"Hello, baby," Ben Phillips said. "Let me get you a chair."

"I'm not staying," Judy said. "I've got to go change." She looked down at Murray, not even saying hello.

"You two know each other?" Ben Phillips said anxiously. "Sure you do. You know Judy, Sam."

Vernon Vernon said thickly, "Pleasure."

"Man, you're drinking too much," Phillips said to him.

"Going to have more," Vernon said. "And more. And more after that."

"Fannell isn't around yet," Judy said to Sam coolly. "I'll let you know when he gets here."

"He doesn't want to meet Fannell," Ben said to Judy. He turned to Sam. "Man, you don't want to meet Fannell."

"Just to say hello," Sam said. He smiled up at Judy. "You look fine."

"Thank you. You look like somebody hit you over the head."

"Somebody did."

"What I like above all," Ben Phillips said, "is a kidder. A good old-fashioned sense of humor. Like Sam here."

"He's a kidder all right," Judy said, but it seemed to Sam her voice was not so sharp as the words conveyed. She looked at him again and said, "I'll see you in a little while," and turned with a bare sweep of shoulder and was gone.

She could not have timed her departure better, because, looking away from her and at the entrance to the room, Sam Murray saw Harry Millburn and his sister Ellie. They were looking around the room. Then Millburn saw Murray and waved a finger, and they came over to the table.

"'Evening," Sam said to Millburn. He stood up and smiled at Ellie. "Hello, you."

"Hi, mister," Ellie said.

"Mr. Phillips," Sam said. "Mr. Millburn and Miss Millburn."

Ben Phillips stood up. "And Mr. Vernon," he said. "I'm sorry about his condition, I really am, but—"

"Gloria!" Vernon Vernon said drunkenly, staring at Ellie Millburn. "I thought the date was tomorrow."

Harry Millburn said sharply, "What's the matter with him?"

"You know our pal here?" Murray said to Ellie.

She shook her head. "He must think I'm someone else."

A doubt came to Sam Murray's mind; once again, he thought of the front page of the morning paper and what it was on that front page that could have disturbed him.

It's like in the army, he said to himself. *If you want to recognize somebody, always send for a drunk eye doctor.*

CHAPTER THIRTEEN

"THE TROUBLE WITH THAT AIMERLY SITUATION," WALTER Lord said to Miss Case, his secretary in the headquarters of the state anti-crime commission at Port Gerard, "is probably mainly Sam Murray. You know Sam."

Miss Case, who was thirty years old and not too bad to look at, said that she knew Sam.

"He gets in a town," Lord said, "and the next thing you know it's like the Fourth of July."

"That's what he's supposed to do, isn't it?" Miss Case said. "Stir things up? Make headlines?"

"Right," Walter Lord said unhappily. "Right, right, right. The thing of it is, though, when we did that job on the docks, it was here in Port Gerard, where you've got three daily papers and all the radio and television time you need. You know, you spread it around. Sam was great. Two newspapers and one radio station won public-service awards for the work he did on exposing the thing on the docks. But the thing of it is—" Lord clasped his hands behind his head and leaned back in his chair—"Sam *knew* the situation here beforehand."

"He always knows the situation beforehand," Miss Case said dryly.

"Ah," Walter Lord said. "But in this case he didn't know the *people*. Now, you take Andy Fannell. I know Fannell. I've messed with him. Sam hasn't. He's moving in on Fannell's territory without knowing anybody there. And that's a tough little burg, that Aimerly. Don't kid yourself." An idea came to him. "Get me the file on Aimerly County."

Miss Case went and got the file on Aimerly County. It was an impressive file. Walter Lord started going through the papers. On top was the resume of the situation that had caused him to send Sam Murray into the town.

Fannell's county; controls loading platforms, some building, may be moving into trucking unions. D.A. Thomas has private practice also. Thomas's judge, E. Yorty, shot and killed, no arrests. Thomas's man opposing alderman candidate Phillips who's talking up shooting and crime. Yorty big wiretap-order man; signed 850 orders last nine months. Yorty, Thomas, Fannell all got along, due mainly presence Thomas's chief investigator Yaros who now dead (natural causes). Thomas planning wait out election before new chief investigator appointed. Good time move in. Only public issue is wiretapping, but good one. Try get much publicity here, interest state legislature. Also can use as lever to expose local corruption. Watch also local race track, Forest Downs, also controlled Fannell. Files indicate much profit-taking here. Local paper Aimerly Times, *television station WACX-TV. Radio station WACX amounts to nothing. Paper, TV run by publisher Leclerc. Good record....*

Walter Lord looked out into space for a time. Then he said to his secretary, "Is there a thing in here on who controls how much stock in that race track?"

"I think so," she said. "Do you want me to try to find it?"

"I've got it here. I'll look." Lord moistened his lips. Then he came to it. Looking at the list he said, "Oh, hell."

Miss Case looked at him with concern.

"A fellow named Millburn," Lord said. "Harry Millburn. Fifty shares. Damn it."

Miss Case said, "Why damn it?"

"Because I don't make any sense," Lord said. "I go to expense to get hold of a secret list like this one and then I go to more expense to authorize Sam to pay this guy Millburn some money out of the confidential fund, because Millburn's a big wiretap man and maybe he can help Sam out, and it never occurs to me to tie in the names on this lousy list. Fifty shares for Millburn. Fannell's got the track. How does Millburn get hold of this stock except he's a friend of Fannell's?"

"I don't understand it a hundred per cent," Miss Case said, "but it sounds like a typical Sam Murray adventure."

Walter Lord let go a low whistle. "And look at that! Three hundred shares to a Mrs. R. Hanner. Now who the hell is Mrs. R. Hanner?"

"Don't look at me," Miss Case said.

"Well, let's find out," Lord said. "Even if he didn't know we'd got hold of this list, Fannell wouldn't be so dumb as to pay off a doll that way. Or would he?"

"I don't know," Miss Case said.

"No," Lord said. "Fannell's too smart. Mrs. R. Hanner is our mystery lady in the balcony, doctor. Now, who the hell would that be?" He moved further into the Aimerly file. "Rape," he said, "extortion, collusion. Conspiracy. Fraud. Union racketeering. Grand jury irregularities. Ah. More rape. Scandal in the police department. Scandal in the fire department. Reorganization of the sheriff's office." He looked up. "And no Mrs. R. Hanner."

Miss Case said, "Do you want to check on her?"

"Yes, damn it," Lord said. "Right away. And send a telegram to Sam Murray, Kamm Hotel, Aimerly. Got your notebook? All right. 'Millburn has—' No. Wait. Strike that. The guy at the telegraph office in Aimerly is probably in on it, too. Make it—" He thought for a moment; then, remembering his phone conversation with Murray earlier in the day, he brightened. "Make it 'Brother of sister has fifty shares stock Forest Downs. Regards.'"

"That ought to help him," Miss Case said.

"By the time it gets to him," Lord said, "probably nothing will help him. You know Sam."

CHAPTER FOURTEEN

"PERSONALLY," ALF HAZLITT, THE YOUNG POLICEMAN, said to his wife Anne, "I think we should vote for Phillips. Wight rife?"

"Hight rusband," Anne said serenely. They were sitting in their living room; the children's toys had been picked up and the missing half of the truck located.

"The word's around the station house to vote for the other man," Alf said, "but I don't know. He seems to me something of a machine man."

"Nobody knows how you vote when you go into the little booth," Anne said. "We've got voting machines here now."

"Finally." Alf nodded. "I just as soon see some of the goings-on in this town come to an end. If it wasn't for that fellow Murray from the crime commission, we'd have never heard anything about that raid on the wiretap operation."

"He must be a nice man," Anne said.

"He is," Alf said. "Two hundred dollars doesn't grow on trees."

"Alf," Annie said, "I don't know. I don't know if it was the right thing to do."

"What? Take the money? Honey, it was a transaction, that's all. That's how an anti-crime commission gets a lot of its information. It pays for it."

"It doesn't sound right."

Alf spread his palms upward. "It's not tainted money. The money comes from the top citizens in the state. Bankers, lawyers, doctors, publishers. They're the ones who keep the anti-crime commission going."

"I know," Anne said doggedly, "but what if he tells them— I mean the police or somebody—that you're the one he got his information from?"

"If he did that," Alf said, "your husband would be in a considerably more delicate situation than you are. An interesting condition, I think they call it."

Anne said, "Aren't you worried?"

"Nope. I've got two hundred dollars I didn't figure on getting hold of otherwise, and you've got a doctor's bill that is now going to be paid. It isn't that hundred thousand I was thinking about, but it's not bad for a start."

"I mean," Anne said, "about this man Murray telling them where he found out those numbers."

"He won't tell them."

"What makes you so sure?"

Alf Hazlitt pursed his lips. "Because," he said, "that's the only thing that keeps an anti-crime commission in business—effectively in business, anyway. Protection of information. If they can't protect their sources, who'd ever tell them anything?"

"Maybe they can make him tell his source."

"I don't see how."

"I don't know," Anne said. "A grand jury or something."

"So he goes in front of a grand jury," Alf said. "So what? He's in business to give information, not to withhold it. So long as he's not withholding anything, why are they going to ask him his source?"

"Only," Anne said, "if the information he's got embarrasses somebody who can tell the jury what questions to ask."

Alf looked at her. She continued, day in and day out, to surprise him—as a woman, as a wife, as a person. He realized that, even though she was doing it on the spur of the moment, she had thought this through further than he had. He bit his lip. There *were* unpleasant possibilities—and two hundred dollars wasn't worth some of them.

He said lightly, "Honey, I'll tell you what. You're married to a cop, but right now he's an off-duty cop. What say we get Doris to sit with the kids and you and I'll go out someplace. Dancing. Something to eat. Tonight we'll be Marge and Gower Champion."

"Can we afford it?" Anne said. "Can we spend the money?"

"Why not? If I lose my job with the police force I can always turn professional informer."

"Funny fellow," his wife said. "Where did you have in mind?"

"Dunno. Like to try the Holiday Inn? Live it up?"

"That's run by that gangster," Anne said. "What would an off-duty cop be doing there?"

"All the cops go there," Alf said defensively. "Matter of fact, I'd like to get a look at that Andy Fannell. Just across the room, maybe, but I'd like to see what he looks like. My brother's a loader, you know, and Fannell runs the store. Like to see what the big man looks like."

Anne shook her head. "If you really want to go out, we'll go to the spaghetti place. Let the Holiday Inn stay where it is."

Alf looked unhappy. "How you going to dance at the spaghetti place?"

"They have a juke box."

"I don't mambo."

"They've got other kinds of records, too."

"Sure," Alf said bitterly. *"Springtime in Aimerly."*

CHAPTER FIFTEEN

IT WAS SPRINGTIME IN AIMERLY, AND MIGHT, TONIGHT, HAVE been spring by almost any standards. There had been an abrupt change in the weather. The lady on the television with her chart and pointer could show where this cold front had made way for that warm front, where this low-running layer of cold moist air had yielded to that high-lying layer of warm dry; but whatever, there was peace on the spacious veranda of the Holiday Inn, and the night was not cold, and the moon shone without clouds over the empire of Andy Fannell, the ruler of Aimerly County.

The empire was not displeasing to see. The Holiday Inn was atop the most commanding of three ridges that parenthesized the city to the west; this was the central ridge, its elevation nearly nine hundred feet, and the lights of Aimerly to the east shone quietly under the stars. It was not, when properly viewed, a bad town. No town was a bad town.

Aimerly had many things, including a recondite record of municipal graft and corruption, but including; too, the best traffic safety record for a city of its size in the entire northeast. Relatively speaking, its schoolteachers were well paid; the utility services were good. Aimerly City Hospital was the finest within one hundred miles, the finest this side of Port Gerard, and its emergency ambulance service was by itself a magnificent thing, and a watchword in that particular trade throughout the country. If you saw a man lying in the street, the ambulance would be there in minutes. Some times, as in the case of Judge Yorty, it took a while before anybody noticed him lying there, but those were exceptions rather than the rule, and besides, in Judge Yorty's case it wouldn't have made any difference.

By now, when he came out on the veranda with Ellie Millburn, Sam Murray had forgotten at least that his head hurt. Ellie tonight was something to see. She wore a gray suit with an extremely tight skirt, and seemed in a more serious mood than she had last night.

"I moved out," she said to Sam.

"Out of where?"

"The apartment."

"Where to?"

"Harry moved me," Ellie said. "I mean, it was his idea. He's rented a room for me here."

"Here?"

"The Holiday Inn," Ellie said. "It *is* an inn, you know. I mean, they have rooms."

"Oh? What was the idea?"

"Nerves. Harry's nerves. My nerves. They won't leave us alone."

"The police?"

She nodded. "One of them followed us out here tonight."

"How can the cops be so sore at one guy? What's he done that's so bad?"

"It's what he hasn't done," the girl said. "What they wanted him to do, and he said no."

Murray shrugged. "So he didn't pay off."

"You told me you were a police detective once," Ellie said. "Didn't you ever run into a policeman who made things miserable for whoever wouldn't play ball?"

"That was in Port Gerard. That's a big city."

"The smaller the city, the worse it is."

Murray looked at his watch. He said, "Technically, I'm supposed to be here to get to meet Fannell. Why, I don't know. What good it'll do me, I don't know. I'm glad you showed up."

She turned and moved into his arms. "Oh, Sam," she said.

They kissed at length, alone on the veranda of the Holiday Inn. When at last Ellie drew back her head Sam looked down at her and said, "That what they teach you at the Missouri School of Journalism?"

"Where?" she murmured.

"The Missouri School of—Oh."

Her brow became furrowed. "What is it?"

"I know what it was now."

"What what was?"

"You write the women's news for the paper," Sam said. "Right?"

"Oh," Ellie said. "That. Yes. But not under my right name."

"It wasn't the name," Sam said. "It was the front page of the paper this morning. Something kept bothering me about it and I never figured out what it was till just this minute."

"Did they get something wrong about the wiretap story?"

Sam shook his head. "It wasn't the tap piece. It was the rest of the front page. The Ladies' Flower Exposition opened yesterday, and a woman had a baby, and there was school news of one kind or another, and on top of all that a real big piece about how the daughter of the police chief gets married."

"I don't follow you," Ellie said, looking at him carefully. "What is it that bothered you?"

"Well, all this stuff that happened yesterday," Sam said. "It's women's news. The kind of thing they send you out to cover. Right?"

"Yes," Ellie said. "So—"

"So how come yesterday was your day off?"

"My day off?"

"That's what you told me. When Harry introduced us in the bar. Of all days for the women's writer on the paper to have a day off."

Ellie began to laugh. "And that's been bothering you all day?"

"Not particularly."

"You're wonderful," she said to him. "Come on."

"Where are we going?"

"I don't know where you're going. I'm going upstairs."

"Where upstairs?"

She turned her head and regarded him gravely. "My room."

"Oh," Sam said. He moistened his lips, and his hand passed in front of his face and began to rub at his ear. "What for?"

"So I can change. That drunk who was at your table spilled some of his drink on me. I smell like a brewery."

"Oh," Sam said again.

"If you're still worried," Ellie said, "the newspaper here has a union just like any other paper. Tuesdays and Sundays are my days off. Yesterday was Tuesday."

"Oh," Sam said again.

"You're still worried?" She stopped at the door that led from the veranda to the lobby of the Holiday Inn.

"A trifle," Sam said.

"What now?"

"Whether it's all right for me to go up to your room with you."

"I'm a big girl now," Ellie Millburn said. There was something in her eyes when she looked at him. "There's a smaller room off of my room," she said. "And a bath. Where I can change."

"Oh," Sam said for the fourth time. He told himself he had the makings of a dirty old man.

His arm was over her shoulder and her arm around his waist as they climbed the stairs. This was one of two flights of stairs that led to the second floor; another flight, just inside the main entrance to the inn and spiraling over the checkroom, led to the gambling rooms upstairs.

But Sam and Ellie found nothing more exciting than a long hallway, elegantly carpeted, with the doors to rooms on either side. Ellie stopped at the last door on the left and went into her purse for her key. The door opened on a room that had a large double bed, a night table with a radio, an armchair, and a chest of drawers. To the left were two doors, on either side of the bed; ahead and along the right side were windows—it was a corner room—and on the same wall as the door to the outer hall, but over toward the right, was another door that led to a large closet occupying the space, Murray assumed, back of where the outer hall ended.

"You," Ellie Millburn said to Murray, "make yourself comfortable."

"How?"

She came over and kissed him briefly. "The night's young yet."

"And you're so beautiful."

"Flatterer."

"Did you ever bend to kiss the sun?"

"What?"

"A line," Murray said, "from a song."

"I want to go downstairs and dance for a while," Ellie said.

"Why don't you meet me down there? While you're changing I'll go on down and see if I can find Fannell."

"You can see him when we both go down," Ellie said.

"That doesn't make much sense. If I can do it now."

"I like the thought of you being out here while I'm changing in the next room," Ellie said. She kissed him again. "I'm wanton."

Sam Murray scratched his ear. "You're sure you—"

She placed a finger on his lips. "You sit there. I won't be long." With a final look at him, she went through the far door on the left-hand wall. That, Murray told himself as he sat in the armchair, would be where the dressing room and bath were. He noticed Ellie had not closed the door all the way shut, had left it open maybe an inch or two. For some reason, he was glad Ellie had wanted him to stay here, now. Maybe it was her way of saying she wanted to go downstairs again while meaning she did not want to go downstairs again—or at least not for a while. Sitting there in the chair, he felt a shiver in his back. *You,* he told himself, *are a pervert or something.*

Yes, he replied to himself, *and isn't life grand?*

There was a rustling sound from the room where Ellie was. Sam swallowed and rubbed his ear and looked around the room. Working for an anti-crime commission was, he told himself at scattered disenchanted moments, the perfect outlet for anyone who was a born snoop. He stood up and gazed out the window for a time; there were two sash windows on each of the corner sides of the room, and a set of draw drapes for each.

He faced the doorway to the inner room and said, "Ellie?"

"Yes?"

"What would happen if I closed these window drapes?"

"Go ahead."

Sam became tight in the throat and drew closed the drapes. The words of the Rodgers and Hart song came to him, and he sang, low and off-key,

> "Isn't it romantic?
> Soon I will have found...."

He thought some basic, non-adoring thoughts about the girl in the next room. Then he took off his coat and placed it carefully over the back of the chair.

A born snoop, he told himself, and walked around the bed and put a gentle finger pressure on the door there, and it opened to reveal a smallish closet. There were a number of dresses and pairs of shoes, and, on the shelf, two hat boxes.

Still humming from the song, he closed the closet door and went to the side of the room where the other two doors were, the one to the outer hall and the other one that must lead to the recessed space beyond the hall.

"Ellie?" he called out.

"Yes?"

"You didn't lock your door."

She laughed. "I trust you."

"I mean the door here to the hall."

He heard the sound of her laughter again. "Lock it if you want to."

"It's up to you," he called. There was no immediate reply, and he added, "If the police are after you like you say, you want to be safe."

"Good idea," she called, and then, the sound muffled by two intervening walls and what he assumed was at least one fully-closed door, he heard her turn on the shower.

"That must have been some whisky the eye doctor spilled on her," he said to himself, but was hardly displeased at the thought of Ellie Millburn taking a shower.

And he bolted the door from the inside.

> "Isn't it romantic?
> Music in the night…."

And noiselessly he opened the next door and looked in.

It was indeed a closet, a big one, of more than even walk-in size, measuring some ten by five feet. It was totally empty of clothing, luggage, or accessories, but there was some furniture—two straight-backed chairs, side by side against the far wall in the darkness to the left, and, straight ahead, a television set on a rolling table.

"Well," Sam Murray murmured to himself. "Come to the Holiday Inn. Television in every room." The thought made him grin. "That son of a bitch Fannell. Television in every room, but you've got to pay your dollar a night for it. Otherwise they keep the set in the closet. What's Fannell got? A million dollars. But a dollar a night extra for television. *Isn't it romantic?* Or maybe he gives the television dollars to the nephew for letting him use his name for the license." His eyes were becoming accustomed to the dark of the closet. "The nephew's probably a bellhop here. He gets an extra dollar tip for wheeling the set out of the closet into the room for you and plugging it in."

He went back into the room, listening to the sound of the shower and wondering whether he ought to send down for some whisky. Then something occurred to him, and he turned and went back to the big closet and looked in again.

There, in the closet, the set *was* plugged in.

CHAPTER SIXTEEN

BILL MACY, A BIG MAN, RED OF FACE, CAPTAIN OF THE confidential squad of Aimerly's police department, sat at the bar in the Kamm Hotel and stared moodily in front of him. His companion was Joe Thomas, the county prosecutor. They were alone at one end of the bar.

"Don't mess with me. Joe," Macy said now, for the third time. "Just don't mess, that's all."

"Nobody's messing," Thomas said mildly.

"I wasn't born yesterday," Macy said. "If you want, I'll reconstruct it for you one last time. Just to make you feel smart and clever all over again."

"You'd better have another drink," Thomas said. "There's nothing to reconstruct."

"Oh, yes," Macy said. "Yes, there is. Because it involves *me*, that's why. And I'm not going to be messed with." He picked up his Scotch and soda but then put it down again and turned to face the district attorney. "This is how it works. You're a district attorney, but you've got your own private law practice, too. And till somebody killed him you had a judge who'd sign any wiretap court order one of your flunkies handed him. He never even looked at what he was signing. He wanted to be protected, too. If it was Andy Fannell's phone and Fannell came back at him, the judge wanted to be able to tell him, 'Andy, I didn't know it was you. I signed it but I never read it.' That's how it was, wasn't it?"

"You're upset, Bill," Thomas said.

CHARLES EINSTEIN

"Goddam right I'm upset," Macy said. "Somebody either came to you in your private practice or you owed some people a few favors—either way, I don't know. But there was some wiretapping to be done. That girl singer—she runs with Phillips; maybe you wanted something on him—and that company that's got something to do with uranium, and the biggest stock brokerage in town. Business information. The only home phone you tapped was the girl's. The others were all business phones."

"Some day," Thomas said, "I'll tell you where—"

"You'll tell me tonight," Macy said, and tapped himself heavily on the chest. "Because you're not going to mess with me, Joe. That was one smart idea too many. You rigged up an affidavit from *my* office saying *I* wanted those phones tapped and then you ran it over to old Judge Yorty and he signed the damn things without even looking, like he always signed them. You wanted it legal, but you didn't want it done through a regular police tap, so you picked the one way of doing it both ways. You had the affidavit come from the confidential squad, because once in a while we do work outside of regular police taps, and that way you got two employees from the phone company to set up the place and they didn't think anything was wrong. And here you go. You're in business. You're protected nine ways from Sunday, even if the worst possible thing happens, which is for somebody at the phone company who's got a friend or two to talk it up a little bit. Which is what happened, and *my* squad gets a tip on it and my own goddam detectives raid the place and what do they get told? *I* was doing the tap! Who helped you with the mechanics? Harry Millburn? He'd tap his mother's phone for a quarter."

Joe Thomas communed with his drink, then signaled to the bartender. "What I don't buy," he said, "is what you're worried about."

"I'm worried about a police report linking those orders to me."

"I've never seen a police report that worried you before."

"When it goes to a grand jury it worries me. Somebody I don't even know, except I've heard about what he's done, this joker Murray from the commission, comes into somebody else's town and the next thing you know all hell's broken loose."

"And Mr. Murray's going to catch most of it," Thomas said. "Don't forget. I've got him in front of the jury tomorrow. I'm going to be the one who asks the questions."

The bartender brought another round of drinks, and Bill Macy contemplated the several shades of difference among truth, the truth as Mr. Sam Murray of the anti-crime commission knew it, and the truth as the grand jury, guided by the questioning of witnesses as regulated by Joe Thomas, might decide. The possibilities were intriguing, and the thought of them mollified Bill Macy.

"Well, I hadn't thought of that," he admitted.

"There, now, you see?" Thomas said agreeably. "If anybody winds up in any jackpot—besides Murray, I mean—why, it'll be those fellows from the phone company."

"They were acting on a court order," Macy said. "They're in the clear."

"No," Thomas said. "I'm not admitting a thing to you, Bill. Let's have that understood. But it's my understanding that while those phone company employees were shown the court order signed by the judge, they were taking the work strictly on their own. You know. Make a little extra money on the side."

"And Harry Millburn was the tap broker and paid them. Who paid him?"

Thomas shrugged. "The point I'm making is that ordinarily, a copy of a court order for a police wiretap has to be filed with the phone company. It's my understanding that they don't have any such copy in their files."

"Well, the damn judge signed one."

"If he did, nobody knows it but him. And he wouldn't—ah—think of talking."

CHAPTER SEVENTEEN

"HEY, ELLIE!" SAM MURRAY CALLED OUT, BUT SHE WAS still in the shower and could not hear him. He stared at the television set in the closet and then stepped in and turned it on.

For a time he saw nothing but dancing lights and patterns; then he turned the channel selector a notch. He had known that the local television station in Aimerly, WACX-TV, was on Channel 8, but what he had here was Channel 4, and he was getting perfect reception. Then he realized that this was one of those small-city areas that had their own UHF channels. What was coming over the television now was some kind of network show, Murray felt sure, for there were many actors, grouped around what he gathered to be a dice table. From time to time the figures of waiters and other people passed directly in front of the camera, momentarily obliterating the view.

"Realism," Sam Murray said, and kept watching. The thing of it was that nobody said anything that made any sense. Sam could hear the voices, but the play had no movement, no dramatic action. It was just footage around a crowded dice table, and nothing else happened.

"Pay-television is the coming thing," Murray said, and switched the channel selector again. What he saw this time was a bedroom scene—only there was nobody in it. It was with eerie sensation that he switched channels one more time. This time his mouth opened and he stared. The camera was looking at a direct, close downward angle at a woman who sat at a make-up table.

Sam could see that she wore a strapless brassiere and a half-slip and nothing else. She took the mascara brush away from her eye, and when the hand moved from her face he saw that the woman was Judy Chasen.

CHAPTER EIGHTEEN

OLD LECLERC, THE PUBLISHER OF THE AIMERLY *Times,* drank too much and smoked too much, in fealty to a theory that since nicotine constricted the arteries and alcohol dilated them, good health depended on balance rather than moderation. As a newspaperman he was not unusual in this respect, but it established a deceptive appearance nonetheless. The fact was that he was a good newspaperman.

Tonight, working on tomorrow morning's edition of the *Times,* he had expected to hear by now from Sam Murray. But no word from Murray had come, and Leclerc was, at the moment, thinking about something else. His printing plant had an order to do sign mats for the school district. Signs like:

UNLAWFUL

TO PASS

STOPPED SCHOOL BUS

FROM EITHER DIRECTION

"It looks lovely," Leclerc said, gazing at the proof sheet for the sign. Then his phone rang, and the girl told him it was a Mr. Walter Lord, calling long-distance from Port Gerard.

Leclerc took the call. "Yup?"

"Leclerc?"

"Yup."

"Lord. Managing director crime commission. Murray's been in touch with you."

"Not tonight, he hasn't."

"Me either. I expected to hear from him."

"What can I tell you?" Leclerc said.

"Matter of fact," Walter Lord said, "you can tell me a number of things. Number one is this: Who is a Mrs. R. Hanner?"

"Who? I don't know. Spell it."

Lord spelled it for him. "Before this is through," he said, "I may have a story for you on the race track over there. There's a road running to the track, you know."

"So I assume," Leclerc said.

"It doesn't run anywhere else," Lord said.

"No?"

"No. It's still a county road."

"So it is," Leclerc said.

"That road-building program in Aimerly County might make fascinating reading for your customers," Lord said. "Ah," Leclerc said.

"Meanwhile," Lord said, "I want to find out about a Mrs. R. Hanner."

"Okay," Leclerc said. "Anything particular you want to know?"

"Everything," Lord said. "And damn fast."

"Done," Leclerc said. "What else?"

"What do you know about Harry Millburn?"

"The name's familiar."

"It should be. His sister works for you."

"She does?"

"Murray told me she does. Doesn't she?"

"Well, wait a minute," Leclerc said. "Millburn—She—oh, my God."

"What?"

"Harry Millburn's a private detective."

"I know that," Lord said irritatedly.

"His sister works with him," Leclerc said. "She's the biggest lay in town."

Walter Lord said, "Oy vey ist mir."

"I beg your pardon?" Leclerc said.

"That——Murray," Lord said. "He's done it again."

"I'll tell you a story," Leclerc said. "I just now heard from a fellow I know who met Sam Murray. This guy was just up here. Murray's out at Fannell's place. The Holiday Inn. I've been waiting to hear from him."

"So?" Lord said hopelessly. "What's the story you're going to tell me?"

"This guy is an optometrist," Leclerc said. "An eye doctor. His wife's left him, and I just now pieced the story together. He saw Murray with a girl. Out at the Holiday Inn. The girl is somebody who comes to this eye doctor for glasses or something. She says her husband's left her, and the next thing you know they've got a date. He's drunk, this optometrist, see? But he says the girl's name is Gloria, only there's a big thing when he tries to say hello to her at Fannell's place and all of a sudden she's with Murray and her name *isn't* Gloria. So what are they going to do?"

"They'll go to the motel," Lord said tiredly, "and at the big moment in rushes the husband with the manager of the motel and the man with the camera."

"Ah," Leclerc said. "Ah."

"Don't tell me," Lord said. "This is Millburn's sister."

"She works with Harry," Leclerc said. "She's got the reputation."

"Does Sam know any of this?"

"He finds those things out, I'm sure."

"You haven't heard from him?"

"No."

"Trouble there," Walter Lord said. "Trouble there. God save the queen."

"Of course," Leclerc said, "this optometrist fellow could have been wrong. He's drunk as hell."

"No," Lord said, in a voice of utter resignation. "No. This is the play. This is the play, all right. Let me tell you something, Mr. Leclerc. Every one of us has a cross to bear. Mine is named Sam Murray."

"Seems like a damn fine chap to me," Leclerc said. "A good man."

"He is," Lord said tiredly. "That's his main trouble."

"Must like girls."

"Yup."

"I've got to be with him," Leclerc said. "I've got to say he's all right."

"Me too," Walter Lord said. "What'd you say this obstetrician's name was?"

"The optometrist?"

"Yeah. Him."

"Vernon," Leclerc said. "Vernon H. Vernon."

"What?"

"Vernon H. Vernon."

"Sure," Walter Lord said.

CHAPTER NINETEEN

SAM MURRAY, NO GENTLEMAN, WATCHED IN FASCINA-
tion as Judy Chasen returned the mascara brush to her
eyes. Yet it was not an issue of propriety that kept him at the
television set in the closet. It was something else, and the real-
ization that went with it.

He heard the shower stop, and he stepped back out into the
bedroom, leaving the closet door open, leaving the television on.

His life, he reflected uncertainly, was an exquisitely balanced
nothing—a superiority of common sense, motive, and intellect
countered on the other hand by the helpless jettison of these
qualities in the presence of a pretty woman. It had happened to
him before and during his marriage, had happened since, and
now was happening again. He knew it was happening, but he felt
unwilling to do anything about it.

Ellie had had a perfectly logical explanation for why she was
not at the newspaper when it seemed she should be at the newspaper. Now, no doubt, she would have a perfectly logical explanation for the television set. She would say, without any question,
that she didn't know it was there—hadn't investigated this closet
at all.

But why would the Holiday Inn have rented this room to
her? Even if they were full up, and had to rent out the room, why
would they leave the set there?

"Hey, Ellie," Sam called.

"With you in a minute," she called back. Then: "You can come in if you want."

He went into the adjoining room, found to his surprise that it was another bedroom almost as big as the main room. This one had its own doorway to the outer hall. His eyes were taking further inventory when Ellie Millburn stepped out of the bathroom.

She said, "Lover, I've changed my mind. I want to do my dancing right here."

He looked at her. She was wearing a white terry-cloth robe, held together, though not necessarily watertight, by a series of oversize buttons and even more oversize button-loops of cloth. She smiled at Sam, then went to the table next to the bed in this room. There was a radio phonograph on the table, and she turned it on. "Music," she said, and smiled at him. "But we'll keep it soft."

Sam Murray sat down on the bed. He said, "You really going to do a dance?"

"Wouldn't you like that?"

Sam scratched his ear. "I suppose I would."

"You suppose? Can't you sound a little more enthusiastic, baby?" The music came up on the radio and she began to move slowly around the room, only walking now but emphasizing the hips. "This isn't the kind of dance you see on television."

"I don't know about that," Sam said.

Suddenly she swung to face him. The top button of the robe came loose beneath her fingers. "Sure?"

"No," Sam said.

"I didn't think so," she said. "But you can be a little more excited, can't you?"

"There are ways," Sam Murray said.

"I know some of them." She came and sat in his lap and undid his tie. "You do my next button."

It seemed to Sam that Ellie talked a great deal. But it was love talk, the kind he didn't mind hearing, and he was down to the last button before he thought again about the television set in the closet off the other room. The old joke with its new punch line—"Those other times you were on television"—came to him suddenly, and he pushed the girl off his lap and stood up and began looking around the room.

Ellie lay on the bed, looking up at him. She said, "What are you doing?"

"Looking for a camera," he said.

"A camera?"

"Yes. What's in there?" He gestured toward a door along the wall where the bathroom wall was.

"I don't know," Ellie said. "Come over here to me, baby."

Sam tried the door. It opened into an adjoining suite. In the center of the room, hunched over a wire recorder with a headset clamped over his ears, was Harry Millburn. There was a tall man with gray hair standing beside Millburn. Both of them looked squarely at Sam Murray, but neither seemed surprised to see him.

Millburn took the headset off. "No camera," he said to Sam Murray.

"No?"

"No," Millburn said. "A microphone serves a much better purpose. A little FM transmitter." Raising his voice, he called out, "All right, Ellie. What we've got is enough. Get back in your clothes." He smiled, pig-eyed, at Murray. "Oh. You wanted to meet Andy Fannell? This is him."

CHAPTER TWENTY

"H E'S GOT A GUN," FANNELL SAID TO SAM MURRAY. "DON'T you, Harry?"

Millburn shifted the end of his cigarette wetly in his mouth and nodded his head. "Here." He patted the shoulder holster inside his suitcoat.

"More important," Fannell said mildly, "he's got a license to shoot one." He said it as if Murray would find this knowledge surprising.

"Let's take it in the other room," Millburn said. He bent over the wire recorder. "We can have a concert."

"The rooms you were just in are our concert rooms," Fannell said. "Did you find the television set?"

"I found it," Murray said.

"You see?" Fannell said to Harry Millburn. He turned to Murray. "Listening, we couldn't be sure whether you'd found it or not." He turned back to Millburn. "Damn your dumb brains anyway."

"Who's he going to tell?" Millburn asked. He lifted up the recorder, leaving the top open. "Come on. I want to play this back."

"After you, Sam," Andy Fannell said to Murray. "I know your buddy Walter Lord. Very well. He came as close as anyone to having me deported. So you can see, this isn't a personal thing, what we've done here. Not that it isn't nice to have this little recording of your voice as far as you're concerned, Sam. Just for preventative purposes, in case you feel like riding your white horse in my direction. What is it they say on those little labels? For the prevention of disease. You're a disease, Sam. You go around pointing your finger at people and saying, 'Look.' That's all you say. 'Look.' A special mission in life. You can't arrest anybody, you can't jail anybody, you can't subpoena anybody. The anti-crime commission. All you know how to do is point your finger. And you feel like you're a very exceptional fellow, because the police won't do it and none of the other authorities will do it, but you boys have no fear. No fear of nothing. Remember that story of the little boy, Sam? The one who watched the parade and all of a sudden pointed with his finger and said, 'Look! The king has no clothes on'? That's you, Sam."

Millburn said, "Let's take it inside."

"I just want to tell Sam one more thing while we're chatting in the doorway here," Fannell said. "Just to remind you one more time, Sam, that it isn't really personal. Basically this isn't something between you and me. Basically it's something between me and Walter Lord. A matter of hate, you might say. But just remember I didn't send for you. You came here on your own."

Sam Murray said nothing, but turned and went into the other room. Ellie Millburn was getting dressed. She wore a girdle and that was all, and was seated on the side of the bed pulling on her stockings, but no one paid any attention to her—except Murray, and his was only a fleeting look.

"Hello, Gloria," he said to her.

"What's that?" Fannell said sharply. "Gloria?" He looked at Harry Millburn.

"Another client of mine," Millburn said. "Nothing that concerns you, Andy. Ellie bumped into the mark tonight and he thinks her name's Gloria. That bit's tomorrow night, isn't it?" This last was addressed to Ellie.

"Yes," she said. "Unless it's loused up by now."

"I don't think it is," Millburn said professionally. "We'll want to use the infra-red for the pictures. Are you going to do it at a motel?"

"Whatever you say," the girl said to him.

"We'll use the same motel we always do," Millburn said. "It's probably a risk going back to the same place all the time, but there's other risks too—finding a new place, breaking in a new motel manager, so forth, so on. The hell with it." He went on into the main bedroom of the suite, and they could hear his exclamation of surprise. "Hey!" he called. "The set's still on in here!"

Fannell said in an even voice, "See anything green?"

"I see Judy Chasen buck naked," Millburn said. "Come here, Andy!"

"You've seen it before," Fannell said tiredly. "Turn it off. We'll be here all night." He turned with an almost apologetic smile to Sam Murray. "You should have realized there wouldn't be any cameras in here, Sam. This is—what would you call it?—headquarters. This is where we look at all the other people. Sometimes we take pictures right off the television."

"Very nice," Murray said.

"Sit down in the chair, Sam," Fannell said. "Don't act so damn martyred. This isn't the only closed-circuit television in the world."

"No," Murray said. "Orwell had one in his book. Big Brother is watching you."

"Ah, but that was 1984," Fannell said, and Murray was surprised that the racketeer knew the book. "Actually, Big Brother's watching now." He sat down on the side of the bed, and the way the light came his face seemed suddenly tired and almost olive dark. "Not here. I mean generally. Some of our finest industries. They wire up the whole plant. Listen in on the union foremen, stick a camera in the men's room, in the place where the shop steward works, the ladies' powder room, anywhere they want. As you said a minute ago, Sam, very nice."

Ellie Millburn came to the door that connected the two rooms of the suite. She was wearing a slip now. She said, "Is it all right if I lie down for a while, Andy. In here?"

"Hey," her brother said to her, "Soon as I can get this plugged in, I'm going to play it back. Don't you want to hear it?"

"Let her lie down," Fannell said to him. He shook his head and smiled at Murray. "Harry's so damn proud of himself every time he bugs a room and gets a recording. He wants the whole world to hear it."

"Well, let's do it," Millburn said. He threw a switch and fiddled with the knobs at the side of the recorder case. The wire wheels began to turn at a great rate of speed, and a squeaky, Betty Boop-ish staccato resulted.

"He's running it backward," Fannell said to Murray. "It only takes a minute to get back to the beginning. Then you can hear it the way it started. I told you he had a gun, didn't I?"

"You mentioned it," Sam said.

"You don't, do you?"

"No."

"Neither do I," Fannell said. "I wouldn't carry one. They're awfully dangerous."

"I'm set," Harry Millburn said. Bent over the portable recorder on the floor he looked over to where Sam Murray was sitting in the chair and grinned. "She's running," he said.

The soundless sound of the moving strand of wire filled the room. Then the voices started. With only sound, without picture or accompanying action, the effect was new and distorted—and could be rerecorded, retaped, reassembled any way Harry Millburn, the expert, desired, to make it more damning yet.

Ellie's voice first: "You make yourself comfortable."

Sam—unquestionably his voice, the wire faithful and without flaw in transcription: "How?"

Ellie: "The night's young yet."

Sam: "And you're so beautiful."

"Flatterer."

"Did you ever bend to kiss the sun?"

"What?"

"A line from a song."

Harry Millburn looked up: "That line can come out."

Now Ellie: "I want to go downstairs and dance for a while."

Sam: "Why don't you meet me down there? While you're changing I'll go on down and see if I can find Fannell."

Ellie: "You can see him when we both go down."

Sam: "That doesn't make much sense. If I can do it now."

Millburn said, "Now he gives in to her. Watch this."

"I like the thought of you being out here while I'm changing in the next room." A pause. "I'm wanton."

Sam: "You're sure you—"

Ellie: "You sit there. I won't be long."

"Now it runs for a while," Millburn said. "What's the matter, Andy? It gets better."

"It's lousy up to now," Fannell said.

"Well, it ain't a whodunit," Millburn said. "You know how it comes out."

"The last part is the only good one," Fannell said.

"What are you worried about? It's my tape got wasted, not yours."

"My money pays for it."

"The charge would have been the same," Millburn said. "Wait a minute. Here we go again."

Here they went again. There was Sam asking Ellie for permission to close the window drapes; Sam asking Ellie for permission to lock the door; then a distant hissing sound.

"Now what the hell is that?" Fannell said.

"My sister taking her shower," Millburn said. "Hear it?"

"That was another bright idea," Fannell said. "What'd she have to take a shower for?"

"She wanted to get him on the bed in that room in there," Millburn said. "Hell, Andy, the transmitter was right under the bed in there. In here, it's in that wall plug. Reception from the bed might not have been as good."

Fannell said, "For this she has to take a shower?"

Millburn shrugged. "This is her business. Let her do it her own way. If she just drags him in here and peels off her clothes maybe he gets upset and runs."

"You wouldn't do a thing like that, would you, Sam?" Fannell said.

"No," Murray said. "Mr. Fannell's right, Harry. If Ellie goes right to work, then I never find that television set."

"Oh, you brain-boy," Fannell said to Millburn. "You mother of all brain-boys."

"Now, wait," Millburn said. "Here it gets good."

Ellie's voice: "You can come in if you want." Then: "Lover, I've changed my mind. I want to do my dancing right here."

More conversation. Then Ellie: "You do my next button."

"Now," Millburn said. He put a cigarette in his mouth.

They listened. "All right," Fannell said when it was over. "A few cuts and it'll be all right."

"The silence is the part I really like," Millburn said.

"So you see?" Fannell said to Sam Murray. "You see what I'm going to add to my record collection?"

"I don't see what good it does you," Murray said. "Who you going to play it for? My wife? I don't have any."

"No," Fannell said. "Oh, no, no, no. I'm not going to play it for anybody."

"Then what's the deal? Why can't a man get laid in peace?"

"No deal," Fannell said. "You can go inside and knock it off right now if you want to. Right, Harry?"

"Why not?" Harry said. "You and me'll watch, Andy."

"No deal," Fannell said again, "unless for some reason it becames a nice thing for the public to learn all about the inner workings of an anti-crime commission. By the public, I mean, of course, that great vehicle the press. We send records to various newspapermen. 'Dear sirs, We thought you would enjoy this transcribed account of how the ace investigator for the anti-crime commission, that great citizens' body devoted to the shining of the public spotlight on wrongdoing of all kinds, goes about his work. We understand the anti-crime commission in this particular case was uncovering evidence in a new drive on whores. First-hand evidence is the best kind, of course. And now we give you Sam Murray.'"

Harry Millburn looked up. "Don't drag Ellie into this."

"No?" Fannell said quietly.

"No," Millburn said. "Christ, Andy, this is my business."

"Well," Fannell said reasonably, "I don't see why Ellie should be dragged into it. The only way Sam could possibly bring in her name would be to tell the story, and it's a story Sam doesn't want to tell. You always protect your source, don't you, Sam?"

Murray said, "Then it is a deal."

"Oh, I suppose," Fannell said. "In a way. But it brings us full circle, Sam. I don't care what you tell anybody about wiretapping. The more the better, so far as I'm concerned—always provided, of course, that you leave Andy Fannell out of it. But it takes us back to the beginning. Maybe next time the anti-crime commission comes to town it won't be wiretapping they're after. Maybe it won't be Sam Murray. Maybe it'll be Walter Lord. Maybe he'll be after Andy Fannell. You see why I want this record, Sam? You understand?"

"Yup," Murray said. "I understand. And what if I quit the commission tomorrow?"

"I'll give you a copy of the record as a going-away present," Fannell said. "As a matter of fact, I'll even give you a job, if you want. There must be something you can do besides point your finger at people. I don't know what you'd do if you were out of a job, do you, Sam? The cops won't have you back. You've been too nasty to them." Fannell laughed. "As a matter of fact, in its own little way this business tonight is a tribute to you, Sam. You ought to be flattered. I'm gambling you won't quit your job. If you don't, I win. If you do, I still win, because the state anti-crime commission will have lost its best man. You like broads, Sam, but you can't be paid off. You can't be bought. How many men do you think there are in the whole wide goddam world like Sam Murray?"

Murray smiled a little sadly. "I can't be bought off?"

"Sure," Fannell said. "Sure. I know. Every man has his price. But when I say you can't be bought off, I'm saying that Andy Fannell doesn't have that price where you're concerned. If I'm right, you tell me. If I'm wrong, I want to know that, too. If I'm wrong I'll have Harry Millburn erase that tape right here and now and we'll talk."

"What about Walter Lord?"

"I've, fought him before and I'll fight him again. He wants to deport me because he can't get me on any other count. I was in jail in prohibition, but I've been out since. I'm going to stay out. In my own way, I'm an honest man, Sam. I'll wipe off that tape right now. Tell me to do it."

Sam Murray rubbed at his ear. "I'd like a drink."

"I'll get you a drink."

"You were right, Andy," Sam said to him. "Whatever it is, Andy Fannell's money doesn't buy it."

"I knew I was right," Fannell said. "I'll still get you a drink. I like you, Sam. What do you think of that?"

"What am I supposed to think?" Murray said.

"He works for me," Fannell said, pointing his finger at Harry Millburn. "He's a slob, but he's goddam good at what he does. Do you know what I do with that television set, Sam? I bring big men out here and every damn room in this place is wired, except these here. Cameras and microphones. You know something?" Fannell took a step toward Murray. "I've never tapped a phone in my life."

"Neither have I," Murray said.

"You and I know how the story goes," Fannell said. "We do our work, each of us in his own way, and we always *can* tap a phone if we feel like it. The ability to do it is always there. When your state legislature investigation gets through with wiretapping, it'll still be there. You know why? Because legislation can't enforce in the business of wiretapping. Science is always five giant steps ahead of the law, Sam. When they invented the automobile, they also invented the getaway car. When they invented the phone, they invented the tap. And each time the cops caught up, those cops were still human beings. The cop that knows what to look for when he looks for a tapped phone can tap a phone on his own."

Murray looked at Harry Millburn. "There aren't any cops after you, are there, Harry? That was all part of the business, wasn't it?"

"I mess with them from time to time," Millburn said. "It wasn't as bad as I made it out to be."

"But you and I," Fannell said to Murray, "know there are other ways to do things besides tapping phones. We don't have to do it. You get your information. I get mine. I use this slob here, and when the big corporation man comes out to the Holiday Inn, we see to it that he has some nice companionship in a bedroom all his own. And then we play him the record, and sometimes we let him watch the television to see the kinds of thing we saw. That way I acquire friends, Sam. Big friends. Stock in corporations. That's how I built my race track."

Sam Murray looked from Fannell to Millburn and back again. Then he said slowly, "But one thing, Andy."

"One tiling? What's that?"

"You can never protect yourself."

"No?" There was understanding between them. "I do pretty good. If I see a gap, I close it up." Fannell gestured with his hand. "Even this local election here. I'm better off if this fellow Phillips loses, because he's got the kind of ambition I don't like. I like the local administration the way it is. But I don't know how people are going to vote. I've got to protect myself. Close the gap. So I let Phillips buy three hundred shares of stock in the track. Strictly as a favor. The price was so low he couldn't say no. I even let him put it in his sister's name. What's that sister's name, Harry? Her married name?"

"Hanner," Millburn said.

"So," Fannell said, turning back to Murray, "you see? I'm protected. If Phillips loses, I'm fine. If he wins, I'm fine anyway because he's not going to take off against any race track."

"What are you telling me this for?" Murray said. "This is the kind of information we pay to get."

"Because I'm protected," Fannell said. "I've got your voice. Sam. I can't buy yon, but I own you. I can't hurt you directly with this recording, but I can discredit anything you try to say. You see the protection? You see what I mean?"

"Yes," Murray said, "but I don't believe it. Millburn here wired the place for you, for pictures and sound. He knows his business. He works for you. And you're so damn dumb you can stand there and say every room in the place is hooked up except this one."

"What do you mean?" Fannell said.

"Ask him," Murray said.

"This slob?"

"That slob."

"Now wait a minute," Harry Millburn said. "I take just so much of this—"

Andy Fannell walked over to him and held out his hand. "Give me the gun, Harry."

"You can go—"

"The gun."

Sam Murray stood up and came over to stand beside Fanned. Millburn looked from one of them to the other. He said, "Christ is my judge, Andy, I didn't—"

"The gun," Fannell said.

Millburn reached into the suitcoat and unsnapped the holster and took out the gun and handed it to Fannell butt end first.

Fannell took it and pointed the gun at Millburn's stomach.

"Show me where the camera is, Harry. The one in here."

"Christ is my judge, Andy."

Fannell socked the point of the gun into Millburn's stomach, and the man gasped. "Where?"

"Christ is—"

"I'm going to shoot you in the hand first," Fannell said. "Then we'll all go inside and talk to your sister about it. You don't think anything of her, but she's a good prop in your work. Now I mean it. Hold up your left hand."

Harry Millburn said, "It's in there." He pointed at one of two air conditioning vents along the wall where the door was to the adjoining room. "There's one to match it for the other room."

"Microphones, too?"

Millburn nodded.

"You were right, Sam." Fannell took the gun away and nodded his head at Murray. "You were right."

"If you knew anything about the English language," Murray said, "you'd know the great line. From Saroyan."

"What Saroyan?"

"*The Propagandists.*"

Andy Fannell stood there, for all the world like a contestant on a quiz program. "I educated myself, Sam," he said. "You think I have no education, but I have. I'm going to tell you the line."

Murray smiled. "I'll start it for you. 'If you listen to them, you will be listened to …'"

Fannell nodded. "'Saying what they said, and no longer the man you were.'"

CHAPTER TWENTY-ONE

FANNELL STILL HAD THE WIRE RECORDING OF THE EPISODE between Sam and Ellie. He had had a bitter scene with Harry Millburn, had left the threat implied that Harry Millburn was going to receive his own due reward, had ordered whisky for Sam Murray, had sent Sam back to the Kamm Hotel in the early hours of the morning in his own, Fannell's, black Cadillac.

But he still had the recording.

"The hell with it," Murray said, and got up out of bed and went inside to shave. He had less than an hour before his scheduled appearance before the grand jury, an appearance to which he looked forward by now with almost a total lack of concern. Now the phone rang and he went to answer it, and it was Walter Lord calling from Port Gerard.

"Boy," Lord said, "am I glad to talk to you."

"I'm not glad to talk to you."

"No? You met Fannell?"

"I met him."

"How'd it go?"

"I'm still alive."

"That's a relief."

"The hell it is."

"Oh, oh," Lord said. "Sam's in trouble."

"After a fashion," Murray said.

"This Ellie Millburn," Lord said.

"Doctor," Sam said into the telephone, "you touched a nerve."

"You found out about her?"

"Yup."

"She's nine different kinds of tramp," Lord said.

"I made my nine the hard way," Sam said.

"Don't tell me," Walter Lord said. "I can almost visualize it."

"I believe you," Sam said, "and yet in another way I doubt it. Well. I get one more chance to louse it up. It's grand jury day."

"Don't worry about a thing," Lord said. "We're all in your corner."

"Somebody better watch the referee, then," Sam said. "I'm being murdered to death."

"Never mind," Lord said. "I've been doing nothing but checking. You made it. The state legislature wants to talk to you as soon as you get back."

"Fine." Sam said. "Walter, let me ask you something. If there was a record—you know, a phonograph record—in existence, of me having a time on a bed with a dame." He paused. "Well. What would you do?"

"I'd listen."

"What if Fannell owned the record?"

"Oh," Walter Lord said.

Sam said, "That's what I thought."

"You poor guy," Lord said.

"Wait till the grand jury sentences me to jail for contempt," Sam said. "Then feel sorry for me."

"The grand jury doesn't do the sentencing," Lord said. "That's up to a judge."

"They've got one of those here, too. A spare judge for after the other one died."

"Don't be insolent to the jury," Lord said.

"They're going to ask me my source."

"Don't tell them."

"I won't. Bake a file in the cake."

"Oh, I almost forgot," Lord said. "There's a fellow there named Phillips, running for alderman or something."

"I met him last night."

"Was he at Fannell's?"

"Yes. With a drunk eye doctor."

"Vernon Vernon," Lord said.

"You come to Aimerly and I'll go back to Port Gerard," Sam said.

"Well, watch out for Phillips," Lord said. "He's tied in with Fannell one way or another."

"Yes," Sam said. "He's got three hundred shares of stock in Fannell's track, registered in his sister's name."

"You stay in Aimerly and I'll stay in Port Gerard," Lord said.

"Phillips," Sam said, "is the least of my worries."

"Well, I checked him out," Lord said. "He came from New York. He was arrested down there one time when he was nineteen years old for kiting a check. The guy he was working for dropped the charge and there was nothing else to it."

"Well, let me think," Sam said. "Does that make him ineligible to run for public office?"

"I don't think it does."

"It hurts his campaign, though."

"I don't think anybody up there knows it."

"Neither do I," Sam said. "Besides, it doesn't hurt his campaign that much. Let's be realistic. What is it? So he was arrested and the charge was dropped. How can this kill him?"

"It can't," Lord said. "I just wanted you to know I checked him out and that's all there is on his record."

"There might be a mystery man there," Sam said.

"Who?"

"Phillips's old boss. The one who didn't press the charge."

"He's been dead twenty years."

"I see," Sam said. "Have you anything else helpful to offer?"

"No," Lord said. "Call me when you get out of the jury."

"Will do," Murray said. "Meanwhile get me a good lawyer."

He hung up the phone and went and opened the door to his room, and the morning paper, left by the thoughtful management of the Kamm, was there. Sam picked it up and looked at the front page and found that he was a celebrity. At least of sorts. His name was right there in the headline of the wiretap story, which was given top left display:

ROTARIANS TO INVITE MURRAY

"Where would we all be without the Aimerly *Times?*" Sam said to himself, and read the story:

Daniel K. Bellekamp, special events chairman for the Aimerly Rotary, announced yesterday he will ask crime-busting Sam Murray, assistant manager of the state anti-crime commission, to discuss the question of wiretapping at next Monday's regular luncheon at the Kamm.

Bellekamp's announcement came as county prosecutor Joseph Thomas asked the grand jury to open a probe of the wiretapping scandal uncovered yesterday by Murray, who is in Aimerly from Port Gerard on special assignment.

Murray revealed police had raided a wiretap headquarters which conceivably could record conversation on any telephone in the MAin 3 and PRospect 4 exchanges, but that no announcement had been made by police concerning the raid, nor any arrests made.

Murray termed the discovery of the tap nest "a shocking example of underworld wiretapping throughout the state."

"Now, I never said that," Murray murmured to himself, and rubbed his ear lobe. Then he remembered there was something he wanted to do and went to the phone and said to the operator, "Let me have Prospect 4-8794."

The operator put the call through and the phone rang three times and then Judy Chasen answered.

"Sam," he said. "Sam Murray."

"Oh," she said. "Sam. Where'd you go last night?"

"I was around," he said.

"I didn't see you."

"I saw you."

She took that at face value and did not ask him what he meant. Instead, she said, "I was going to introduce you to Andy Fannell."

"I met him."

"Oh," she said again. Then: "I owe you an apology. For yesterday."

"No you don't," Sam said. He grinned. "I was a beast."

"No. I do. You were willing to help me, and that's more than anybody else was."

"Well," he said, "I wanted to see you about something."

"Oh? What?"

"I'd rather not over the phone."

"Oh," she said again. "All right. Can you come out?"

"I'm supposed to go to the grand jury."

"When will that be over?"

"I don't know. About noon, I guess."

"Why don't you come out then? I'll be here."

"Good," Sam said. "I'll do that. Judy?"

"What?"

"I like the way you sing."

"Thanks, Mr. Man," she said. "I'll be looking for you."

Hanging up the phone, he felt better, though he was not sure why this ought to be. He consulted his watch, looked out the window, put his raincoat on over his suit, and went downstairs and outside into the rain. The doorman offered to get him a cab, but said, too, that the County Court House was only two blocks down. Sam walked it.

They showed him to the grand jury room, and said he was expected. He went right in. He had been in grand jury rooms many times as a detective, but the sight of one never ceased to remind him of a surgical amphitheater, with the jurors seated in tiers running up from the main table in the center of the room and the foreman of the grand jury and the district attorney standing side by side on the topmost tier, looking down at him.

"Samuel Murray?" the bailiff said.

Murray nodded.

Joe Thomas's voice came down from the top of the room.

"Swear him."

CHAPTER TWENTY-TWO

THE SPRING SESSION OF THE AIMERLY COUNTY GRAND JURY numbered twenty-four jurors. Sixteen was a quorum. There were twenty-four here today. They had heard the other evidence, such as two frightened detective witnesses could provide. Now they heard Sam Murray tell them the same things that had been in the Aimerly *Times*.

The jurors fidgeted and waited. There was nothing new here. They watched for Joe Thomas to make his move.

The county prosecutor did not keep them in suspense too long. He said, "Now. Mr. Murray."

"Yes, sir."

"You've told the jury everything you know about this matter?"

"Yes, sir."

"Except one thing, Mr. Murray."

"Yes?"

"The question of who told you."

Murray took a breath. "I'm pledged not to reveal my source."

Thomas nodded and smiled. "You realize the identity of your source is vital to this investigation?"

"No, sir."

"I beg your pardon?"

"I said, no, sir. I don't realize that."

"Well, let me bring you up to date," Thomas said. "Two detectives have already testified before this jury this morning. Both men participated in the raid. Both men said they found only one man, a telephone company employee, actually in the apartment. They said another man was in the hall outside. But according to the papers, *you* said there were two men *in* the apartment. Do you notice a difference?"

"Not one that matters," Sam said. "The police were there. I wasn't."

"How did you get hold of the phone numbers?"

"I'm pledged not to reveal my source."

Thomas turned. "Does the foreman want to ask this question?"

The foreman of the grand jury leaned forward nervously. "How did you get hold of the phone numbers, Mr. Murray?"

"Somebody gave them to me."

The foreman turned to look at Joe Thomas and the prosecutor mouthed the silent words *Ask him who.*

The foreman cleared his throat. "Who?"

"I can't tell you that," Sam Murray said.

Thomas muttered, "Ask him why."

"Why can't you tell us, Mr. Murray?"

"Because," Sam said, "I'm pledged not to reveal my source."

A smattering of learning occurred to the jury foreman, and he carried the ball on his own with the next question. "Are you taking the Fifth Amendment?"

"No, sir," Murray said.

"You're not supposed to take the Fifth Amendment in a Grand Jury proceeding," the foreman said.

"I can take the Fifth Amendment in any jury proceeding in the United States," Sam Murray said evenly.

"Then you *are* taking the Fifth Amendment?"

"No, sir."

"You're not?"

"No. I don't have to. The Fifth Amendment doesn't apply here one way or the other. I'm not testifying against myself."

The foreman looked helplessly at Thomas, and the district attorney gave him a baleful return glance and took over the questioning.

"Let's all get this straight, Mr. Murray. What you're doing, very simply, is refusing to answer a question put to you by the foreman of the grand jury of Aimerly County. Is that right?"

"I suppose so," Sam said.

"You suppose so? Don't you know so?"

"Yes, sir."

"You still refuse?"

"Yes, sir."

Joe Thomas waited a moment. Then he said, "Is it the custom of the state anti-crime commission to co-operate fully with all bodies of law enforcement?"

"Yes, sir."

"Do you believe that a grand jury is part of the machinery of law enforcement?"

"Yes, I do."

"Yet having said you co-operate fully with all bodies of law enforcement, you nonetheless refuse to answer questions put to you by a body of law enforcement. Is that right?"

"When the question has no relevance to the prosecution of the case."

Thomas smiled; his tongue darted out and he wheeled to face the jury foreman. "Do you believe the question you asked, the question Mr. Murray refused to answer, was relevant to the prosecution of this case, or are you in the habit of asking irrelevant questions?"

"Yes, sir, I do," the foreman said hastily. "No, sir, I'm not."

Thomas began to pace the topmost tier, letting his voice ring clear. "Perhaps," he said, and paused, looking around the room, then started in again. "Perhaps it is a small question, after all. Whether the second man was in the apartment or in the hall outside. But after all, that's what we're here to try to discover, isn't it?" He stopped pacing. "Gentlemen of this jury, it is the duty of a grand jury to determine the facts of an issue so it can properly be decided what indictment, if any, shall be handed down, and the nature of that indictment. Protection of information, which seems to be a matter of virtue with Mr. Murray, the witness here, is actually, as all of us know, inherent in a grand jury proceeding which is by its very nature a secret proceeding."

Sure, Sam Murray said to himself, listening to Thomas, *unless it's some poor cop you can hang. Secret from who? You, Joe?*

Thomas's voice had attained a singsong quality. "Yet under the very definition of protection, this witness has his own code. He has his own kind of protection. He seems to think it sets him above the law. The law is clear where it applies to contempt of a grand jury. An employee of a private anti-crime commission, such as Mr. Murray here, is not—I repeat, not—exempt under the law from having to answer the question he has refused to answer. Nor is he exempt from the contempt action which logically must follow such refusal. Now another thing." Joe Thomas rubbed his hands together, almost gleefully, Murray thought. *Ah,* the crime commission man said to himself. *Now he throws the spitball.*

And you could see Joe Thomas spit on the ball before he threw it. "And of especial interest to the grand jury of Aimerly County, gentlemen, would be, I should think, a coincidence. Or let's call it a coincidence. This is the first time our metropolitan area has been honored" (he gave the word "honored" the full stentorian treatment) "by a visit from the state anti-crime commission. The commission professes itself interested in making headlines. I see by the local morning paper that Mr. Murray is going to make a speech at the Rotary Club luncheon next Monday. No doubt we'll be seeing a lot of him on television. But I said coincidence. And we all have to admit it is a coincidence. One day, for the first time in history, the man from the crime commission comes to town. The crime commission has an admirable project—expose illegal wiretapping. I say admirable. So, when you have an admirable project like that, why, you want to bring it to the attention of the people. You need an illustration. And all of a sudden, Mr. Murray's in Aimerly ten minutes and we have a wiretap nest. I'll leave it to you gentlemen of the jury." Thomas seemed suddenly angry. "It's too much of a coincidence for me."

The room was absolutely still. The foreman of the grand jury looked uncertainly at Joe Thomas. Then he cleared his throat.

"Mr. Murray?"

"Yes, sir?"

"Do you want to answer *that* question?"

"What question is that?"

"The question the district attorney, Mr. Thomas here, just asked."

"I didn't hear him ask a question."

"You didn't?"

"No, sir."

"What did you hear him do?"

"I heard him express an opinion."

The foreman looked helplessly at Thomas. The prosecutor took a step forward. "Gentlemen of this jury," he said, "the witness is correct. He's a bright young man, this witness, a very bright boy. If you were in English composition class in junior high school and you wanted a passing grade on your test, you couldn't put a question mark after what I just said. No, technically speaking it wasn't a question. But you know and I know, gentlemen—bright witness or no bright witness—the question is there."

Again the stillness came over the room. Thomas looked cyni-
cally at the foreman of the grand jury and stepped forward again.
"If I may, gentlemen, I would like to suggest that this witness
has several serious decisions to contemplate. It would be well for
him to decide whether he has told us the entire story as he knows
it. If he hasn't, it would be well for him to decide whether he
intends to tell us or not. And finally, it would be well for him to
decide whether he wishes to be confronted by a contempt citation
for failing to answer a specific question." Thomas licked his lips.
"Now, in the interest of fairness all around, gentlemen, would
the jury be willing to ask this witness to return at this same time
tomorrow morning, at which time, having had an opportunity
to consider the very serious decisions he must make, we may find
him more responsive?" The prosecutor smiled sardonically down
at Sam Murray. "That's a question, Mr. Murray, not an opinion."

The jury foreman looked around. Then, helpless as ever, he
croaked, "So ordered."

"I suggest you excuse the witness," Thomas said mildly.

"The witness is excused until tomorrow at the same time,"
the jury foreman said, and nodded at Sam Murray. "Be here."

"Yes, sir, your honor," Murray said, and rubbed at his ear and
went out.

CHAPTER TWENTY-THREE

JUDY CHASEN WAS WEARING A SWEATER AND SKIRT THIS TIME as she waited for Sam Murray at the stair landing, and he got an admirable view of her legs on the way up.

She smiled at him and said, "Hi. Did you eat?"

"No," he said.

"I've got something for you," she said. "Do you like tongue?"

"It so happens I do," Sam said, and followed her into the apartment. He took off his raincoat. "I may cry."

"What? Cry? What for?"

"That's the first nice thing anybody's said to me today," Sam said. "Do I want some tongue."

"Nut," she said to him. "Here. Let me take your coat." She took the coat and went to the hall closet with it, talking to him over her shoulder. "How was the jury?"

"About what I expected."

"Good?"

"No."

She came back into the room. "What happened?"

"I may go to jail."

"Why?"

"Contempt of the grand jury. I wouldn't tell them where I found out what I found out."

"Why not?"

"Because for one thing it isn't material to the case. I told them everything I knew. For another thing, it would get an innocent man in a lot of trouble."

She shook her head. "Come on in the kitchen. Didn't you explain to them that it wasn't material?"

"I tried to."

She opened the ice box door. "They asked you to answer anyway?"

"Yup. District attorney doesn't like crime commissions. Not in Aimerly County, anyway."

"I thought you said this was the grand jury."

"It was. First base, second base, catcher: D.A. pitching."

Judy Chasen reached up a hand and flicked an errant wisp of hair away from her forehead. Sam watched her as she took the food out of the ice box. "You know something," he said, "you have a fresh face."

"A what?"

"Fresh. You know. Well-scrubbed. Clean. Nice."

"Well." The lock of hair fell back across the forehead and Judy tried blowing it back in place, her lower lip pushed out so that she looked like a little girl. She laughed. "That's the nicest thing anybody's said to *me* today."

"While we're trading compliments," Sam said, "I think all of you is very nice."

"Oh?" She stopped, milk in one hand and the butter plate in the other, and looked at him. "Do you have a television camera all your own in my bedroom?"

"No," Sam said. "Andy Fannell has one all his own in your dressing room."

She laughed again.

"I'm serious," Sam said. "I mean it. I wanted to tell you. And you don't know where you heard it. All right?"

She stood there, staring at him.

"See if you don't have an air-conditioning vent up over your mirror," Sam said. "And if you do, either cover it up yourself or raise hell about it. That whole Holiday Inn is wired for sound and closed-circuit television. I caught your act last night, if you'll pardon the expression. By mistake."

Judy sat down in a chair at the kitchen table. Sam Murray had forgotten what a girl looked like blushing, but it was not a displeasing sight to see. She said, "You saw?"

He nodded.

"Everything?"

"No," he said, and pretended to be busy looking out the window for a moment. "But I gather other people have."

"How long has it been going on?"

"I don't know."

"That bastard," Judy breathed.

"Well, it shouldn't be too hard to put a stop to it," Sam said. "I gather your dressing room's a small place. You ought to be able to stop up the chinks."

"They've probably got pictures of me, too," the girl said. "I mean, not television. Regular."

"I'm damned if I know what you can do about it," Sam said. "I did want to tell you about it."

"I'm glad you did," she said.

"If it'll comfort you any," he said, "from what I could find out your dressing room is the last place in the Holiday Inn anybody's interested in. They've got bigger game stashed all over the hotel."

"I've known some of that," Judy said. "But only by rumor. Fannell's never approached me that way."

"Fannell," Sam Murray said, "is a gentleman."

"A funny kind, if you ask me," Judy said.

"We're all funny kinds of gentlemen, in our way," Sam said, and for some reason he became beset by an urge to transform the one most useless bit of information he had picked up—the record of Ben Phillips's arrest in New York years ago—to something for his own advantage with Judy Chasen. To tell Judy this would not help her with Phillips, would not help Phillips with her, might help Sam with her.

"Nuts," he said aloud.

Judy said, "Come on. Sit down. What's the matter?"

"I don't know," Sam said. "There's something the matter with me. I ought to be in the zoo."

"Are you that hungry?"

"No. I was thinking of the reptile house."

"Oh, Sam," she said. "What's the matter?"

"I should be thinking about going to jail," he said.

"What were you thinking about instead?"

"You."

Judy got up to get the bread. As she passed behind him she bent her head suddenly and kissed him on the forehead. Their eyes met at an absurd upside-down angle. They both began to laugh.

"I don't know," Sam said. "I say to myself this must be all right. Belted one day, kissed the next. Slap in the face today, tongue sandwich tomorrow."

She laughed gaily. "The difference, mister. You didn't see the difference."

"What?"

"Yesterday I wore slacks. Today a skirt."

"Which one is your working clothes?"

"I ought to slap you for that," Judy said, but she was not angry. She sat down at the table again. Her voice became momentarily serious. "You do have to protect the source of your information, don't you?"

"Sure," Sam said. "It's a box either way, but you have to do it."

"A box either way?"

"Either way it hurts the crime commission, now. The crime commission can only operate by protecting its informants. If I go to jail it means the law doesn't approve of the way the crime commission operates. The only way I stay out of jail is to purge myself of contempt and give the source. So either way the commission lands on its uppers."

"Isn't there any other way out?"

"I wish I could think of one."

"I can think of one."

He stared at her.

"Suppose I could persuade Ben Phillips to withdraw from the election."

Sam said, "I don't—"

"Wait," Judy said. "You said it's the district attorney who's opposing you, who's run the grand jury up to now. Well, he opposes Phillips, too. It seems to me if Ben could be taken out of the race and somebody told the district attorney it was your suggestion, then he might agree not to press the contempt."

Sam reached out and took her hand in his own. "I don't know," he said, "but I think you're somebody. I really think you're somebody."

"Don't you think the district attorney would go for it?"

"No," Sam said. He brought back his hand and rubbed his ear lobe. "I say 'no.' Actually, I don't know. I guess there's a chance he even might. But that's beside the point. Mechanically, it wouldn't work. It would take several steps, and the first step would be the hardest, and I wouldn't ask you to do it. I wouldn't want you to do it. For one thing, he's got a right to run if he wants to."

Judy said in a dry voice, "There's something he wants more than that."

Sam looked at her, but she would not look at him. At long last, he said slowly, "No, Judy. No."

CHAPTER TWENTY-FOUR

I T WAS AFTER MIDNIGHT OF A DAY NAMED JUDITH CHASEN that the phone rang in Sam Murray's hotel room. Murray had been lying on the bed, half-reading a western, still dressed, and he picked up the phone and lay there with the phonepiece balanced across his neck so he could hear and talk without holding it.

It was Andy Fannell.

"I want to see you, Sam."

"What for?"

"For a ceremony," Fannell said. "I'm going to erase your voice on that piece of wire. You did me a favor last night. I've decided to do one for you tonight."

Sam grinned. "The reformation sets in."

"The reformation sets in," Fannell agreed. "Also there may be some help I can give you on the grand jury thing. I doubt it, offhand, but maybe it's worth talking about. The jail here stinks."

Murray sat up. "All right, Andy. Good. When? Where?"

"I'll send the Cadillac for you," Fannell said.

"Car-dropper," Murray said to him.

Fannell laughed. "No. If I was a car-dropper I would have said I'll send *a* Cadillac for you. I've only got one. It'll be just me and the driver."

"I'll be out front," Murray said. "About forty minutes or so?"

"Forty minutes to an hour," Fannell said.

"Oh," Murray said. "One other thing, Andy. While I've got you on the phone. Something that's been bothering me. Something I meant to ask you last night."

"Yes?" Fannell said. "What's that?"

"So long as you admire me so much, Andy," Sam said, "and so long as you wanted to maneuver me out to that place of yours, then tell me one thing. Why'd you have the fellas hit me on the head?"

"When?"

"Yesterday noon. I got slugged."

"Why'd I have it done?"

"That's what I'm asking."

"I can answer that in two words," Fannell said. "I didn't."

Sam hung up the phone, felt via association to see if his head still hurt—it did if you pressed—and went back to his western, but got nothing out of it. He was thinking too much of his day with Judy, through supper, up to the time when she had to go to work.

At length, some thirty minutes later, he stood up and went into the bathroom and looked at himself sadly in the mirror. Then he put on his coat and went downstairs to wait for Fannell.

The lobby of the Kamm Hotel was absolutely empty. There was no one even behind the desk. Sam looked around, then turned to go out the main door. As he did so, the door opened and Ben Phillips came in.

Phillips stopped short, looking at him. He seemed out of breath. "Man," he said, "you're just the man I've been looking for. I want to talk to you."

"Hello, Ben," Murray said. "Been out to the Holiday Inn?"

"Just came from there," Phillips said. "Judy said you were in trouble with the grand jury."

"She did?"

Phillips nodded. "Yup. And I made a deal with her."

Sam felt his throat constrict. "What kind of a deal?"

"As a favor to her," Ben said, "I volunteered to incorporate this episode into my campaign material." He smiled. "Matter of fact, it'll do *me* a lot of good. You know, Sam." His hand painted the words in the air. "Crime-buster jailed—all he did was expose wrongdoing, and for this he goes to jail—what we need is a change in this town. Wonderful! This can put me over, Sam."

Murray looked at him. "As a favor to Judy, you're going to make campaign material out of my going to jail?"

"This may keep you out of jail, Sam," Phillips said earnestly. "Don't you see?"

"No," Sam said. "I don't. The law is the law."

"Public indignation is a powerful thing," Ben Phillips said. "I want you to tell me the whole story, so I'll know how to present it best to the voters."

"You're really hell-bent for election, aren't you?" Murray said. They had moved toward a settee at the north side of the lobby, but now it occurred to Murray that he should go out on the porch to be there when the car came.

He started to move toward the door to the porch. Ben Phillips got up and followed him. He said, "Man, you don't get me. Why don't you tell me this source of information you're covering up? That Joe Thomas is just aching to make a deal with me. Maybe I could go to him privately, straighten the whole thing out. Then he'd be happy and I'd be happy, and you'd stay out of jail."

Murray thought of the young cop, Alf Hazlitt, and it occurred to him that it was his own insistence that had made Hazlitt accept the money from him, much as he needed it. There were different kinds of honesty, Murray told himself now, and the best kind was Alf Hazlitt's. You never changed the world. Sam would go to jail, and when he got out Aimerly would be pretty much the same place. You would not change Joe Thomas or Andy Fannell, but perhaps you had accomplished something. You had taken care of Harry Millburn. Chalk one for virtue. Millburn was in trouble now, and Fannell would know how to deal with him. The state legislature was, as a result of your visit here, going to investigate the bad business of eavesdropping—and perhaps new laws, affording more on the side of the right, and greater protection for more people, would result. And you were guarding the lifeline of a young policeman whose two great crimes were that he wanted to tell somebody the truth, and that his wife was going to have a baby. Was it really a loss?

Sam said nothing, but went through the door to the porch.

From the porch, there were four entrances to the hotel: the main entrance, another that was little more than a side door at the north end, and then the barbershop and the drugstore, both unnecessarily ornate without being overly so, both having rear doorways that led to the hotel lobby. It was through the small auxiliary door at the north end of the porch that Sam Murray came. He paused there for a moment, seeming to lean his body in the direction of the street light some forty feet away, and faintly in that light, more noticeably in the light from the moon, the old gold railroad watch glistened dully as Ben Phillips, who had come out to join Murray on the porch, took it out to see the time.

"This place gives me the creeps," Phillips said. He looked around nervously. "This is the same door the judge came out of. About the same time of night, I guess. And nobody around." He pointed a shaking finger diagonally down the length of the porch. "That's where they found the body."

"Well, you watch me and I'll watch you," Sam said. "It is kind of unpeopled out here, isn't it?"

"They could have shot the judge in Death Valley," Ben Phillips said. "They wouldn't have had any more privacy."

"Nobody saw it," Sam Murray said, shaking his head; and the rest of the sentence came from his lips before, in all prudence, he had a chance to stop it; "so how do you know what door the judge came out of?"

He turned slowly, but the gun came up in Phillips's hand. "Walk ahead of me, Sam," Ben Phillips said. "Down the porch. Slowly."

Murray turned and began to walk.

"With the hands up," Phillips said.

Murray nodded sadly and raised his hands, walking. He said over his shoulder, "Everything I find out is too late."

"Right," Phillips said.

"Right," Murray said. "You get arrested when you're a kid and nothing comes out of it but you come here and make your living out of a big string of liquor stores. And you have to apply to the State Liquor Authority for a license, and the application has a line on it, 'Have you ever been arrested or convicted?' and you—what? Said no or left it blank?"

"What difference does it make?" Phillips said. "Walk slowly."

"And the judge was the only man in the world who had the brains and the access to the files so he could link the two things up. So he would have shaken you to death. Alderman Phillips. Fraudulent license application. Record of arrest."

"Stop right there," Phillips said.

Sam stopped. From the railroad two blocks away there was the dirty metallic sound of a fast freight, eighty cars or more, twin diesels already long out of sight and gone. It was a rattling sound, the sound of empty freight cars and wheels clacking over the switch points beyond the depot. And almost immediately another fast freight, this one going the other way, hammered the center of the town and was gone; and the other sound, the sound of the gunfire, could have come from anywhere. It chased itself echo for echo, so no one could say there had been four shots instead of two, or one instead of three.

No one? Well, maybe Ben Phillips knew.

CHAPTER TWENTY-FIVE

PATROLMAN ALF HAZLITT, WALKING HIS BEAT ALONG THE side street that flanked the Kamm Hotel, was thinking idly to himself, as he had often today, that Sam Murray was a man of his word. He heard the freight trains as he thought about the way Murray must have stood up before that grand jury. He heard the other sound, too; the other sound came from Rain Street, no more than thirty feet ahead, and as Hazlitt started to run toward the sound of the gunfire, a black Cadillac whipped around the corner from Rain Street and glided swiftly past him.

There were two figures on the sidewalk-porch of the hotel; one standing, one fallen. Hazlitt raced along the porch, and the standing figure turned to face him.

"For God's sake!" Hazlitt panted. "It's Mr. Murray!"

Murray peered at him.

"It's me," the cop said. "Alf Hazlitt. Who's that?"

"Former candidate for alderman Ben Phillips," Sam said. "I think he's still alive."

"Who shot him?"

"I don't know. The shots came from a car."

"I saw it!" Hazlitt said excitedly, bending over the fallen Ben Phillips.

"That's Phillips's gun," Murray said. "It hasn't been fired."

"I tell you I saw the car!" Hazlitt breathed. "It went right by me on the side street."

"I saw it, too," Murray said.

"Then you can corroborate," Hazlitt said. "A black Cadillac. That ought to be easy to—"

Murray looked down at him. Then he said slowly, "No, Alf. We saw the same car, but maybe the light's a little better on Rain Street here. It was a sedan, but I could swear it wasn't a Cadillac. And it wasn't black."

Hazlitt looked blankly up at him. "Do you know who did it?"

Murray shook his head and shrugged. "Nope. My guess would be The Syndicate."

CHAPTER TWENTY-SIX

I T WAS A VASTLY DIFFERENT ATMOSPHERE IN WHICH SAM Murray testified before the spring session of the Aimerly County Grand Jury at ten o'clock in the morning. They were digging the bullets out of Ben Phillips, but he would live. It took the jury very little time to decide upon a verdict of attempted homicide at the hands of person or persons unknown. Also to indict Phillips in the killing of the judge.

Outside the grand jury room, prosecutor Joe Thomas shook Murray's hand. "You're finally leaving town, Sam?"

"Finally?" Murray said. "I haven't been here very long."

"A lot's happened, though," Thomas said.

"I know," Murray said. "And now it looks like I'm going to miss the Rotary Club luncheon."

"I'll be serious with you, Sam," Thomas said. "I was concerned with Phillips in this election, and I don't mind telling you. The judge was a friend of mine, but he kept that business about the liquor license his own little secret, and I'm not sure I blame him. We all like to have that little extra something going for us."

"No doubt," Sam said.

"And the jury won't be needing you when it resumes its investigation into the wiretapping business," Thomas said. "I've talked to the foreman."

"So long as I stay away from Aimerly?"

"Oh, hell, we'd love to have you back any time you want to come," Joe Thomas said. "Just—ah—take care of yourself." He looked away. "A man can get hit on the head only so many times."

"Sure," Sam said. "I should have guessed. Who else would the hotel let into a guest's room?"

"Well," Thomas said. "I just want to ask you one more thing. How did *you* find out the details on Ben Phillips's past?"

"From the state anti-crime commission," Sam said, and nodded, and went out and back to the hotel.

The room clerk signaled him across the lobby. The clerk seemed agitated about something. "Mr. Murray?"

Sam went to the desk. "Something?"

"A gentleman was here," the clerk said doubtfully. "He left you two things. He said to give them to you in order. First this." With great distaste he held up a coil of very thin wire. "Is something funny, Mr. Murray?"

"Sort of," the crime commission man said. "What was the other thing he left?"

"Just this flat package," the clerk said. "He told me to be very careful of it, because it was breakable and a very rare object and the only one of its kind in existence and—" the clerk drew in a breath "—you would have to have it for your old age."

Sam took the package and opened the flap and looked inside. The clerk leaned over the counter. "What is it?"

"A phonograph record," Sam said, grinning.

"Does it have a title?" the clerk said. "I'm a Goodman fan myself."

"Good," Sam said. "This one is *Let's Dance.*"

The clerk looked puzzled. "A fine record, but it's not *that* rare."

"Some of them are," Sam said. "Now when's the next train out of here?"

The next train was less than an hour away, but he made it to the depot with ten minutes to spare. He was standing there on the platform, reading in the Aimerly *Times* about the choice of a site for the Aimerly County Fair, when Judy Chasen came out of the station door. He turned and she ran to meet him, and there was nothing equivocal about it. She kissed him hard.

"That's a silly hat," Sam said to her.

"I'm a silly girl," she said. "Sam?"

"What?"

"I quit my job at the Holiday Inn. I'm going to leave Aimerly."

"Any special reason?"

"You know the reason."

"I don't mean about what went on out there. I mean, is there any special place you're going?"

"No," she said, watching him. "I'm just going home and packing my bags and leaving."

He kissed her again. Then he said, "Port Gerard is nice."

"Sam," she said. Then she kissed him. "I have no shame."

"What's shameful about being Mrs. Sam?"

They could hear the whistle of the oncoming train. Judy looked at him wide-eyed. "Now you're proposing."

He kissed her one more time.

Judy said, "Do you do everything on such short notice?"

"Most everything," he said.

She shook her head in wonderment. "How do you get away with it?"

Sam Murray picked up his suitcase and grinned. "I know a judge."

www.ingramcontent.com/pod-product-compliance
Lightning Source LLC
Chambersburg PA
CBHW052009240626
47153CB00008B/2798